Ethan returned his focus to Addie. "I've found new evidence in your mother's case."

She turned slowly to face him. "What?"

"I wasn't lying when I said I came to Charleston to see you, but I'm also here pursuing a lead. I wanted you to know before you heard it from someone else."

She shoved back a lock of damp hair. "Assuming I believe you, what makes you think I'd ever want any of this dumped on my doorstep?"

"Besides the fact that your mother was murdered? You're a police detective. You must be interested in justice."

She said nothing for the longest time, just stood there staring back at him as he searched her face. Her eyes were so much bluer than he remembered. Softer, too, and liquid. They reminded him of a Monet painting he'd seen in The National Gallery.

But right now, those eyes were narrowed in suspicion. "My mother's case is closed. As far as I'm concerned, justice was served twenty-five years ago when your father was committed to the fourth floor."

"Maybe. Or maybe an innocent man was framed for something he didn't do."

CRIMINAL BEHAVIOR

AMANDA STEVENS

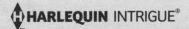

Recycling programs
for this product may
not exist in your area.

ISBN-13: 978-1-335-64085-7

Criminal Behavior

Copyright © 2019 by Marilyn Medlock Amann

Printed in U.S.A.

www.Harlequin.com

Amanda Stevens is an award-winning author of over fifty novels, including the modern gothic series The Graveyard Queen. Her books have been described as eerie and atmospheric, "a new take on the classic ghost story." Born and raised in the rural South, she now resides in Houston, Texas, where she enjoys binge-watching, bike riding and the occasional margarita.

Books by Amanda Stevens

Harlequin Intrigue

Twilight's Children

Criminal Behavior

Pine Lake
Whispering Springs

Bishop's Rock (ebook novella)

MIRA Books

The Graveyard Queen

The Restorer
The Kingdom
The Prophet
The Visitor
The Sinner
The Awakening

Visit the Author Profile page at Harlequin.com.

CAST OF CHARACTERS

Detective Adaline Kinsella—One of Twilight's Children, Addie grew up in the shadow of her mother's brutal murder. She's tried to put the past behind her, but it's hard to move on when the man who broke her heart is determined to set the killer free.

Special Agent Ethan Barrow—Ethan has always believed the wrong man was incarcerated for Sandra Kinsella's murder. New DNA evidence has sent him back to Charleston—and back into Addie Kinsella's life.

Gwen Holloway—A former FBI profiler with a lot to lose.

James Merrick—A legendary profiler who allowed one too many monsters to crawl inside his head.

Deputy Chief David Cutler—His life changed forever the night he found Sandra Kinsella's body.

Helen Cutler—A therapist who knows too many dark secrets.

Daniel Roby—A man with a deadly obsession.

Naomi Quinlan—A murdered genealogist who made an interesting discovery.

Chapter One

Located at the end of a dead-end street, the derelict Victorian seemed to wither in the heat, the turrets and dormers sagging from time, neglect and decades of inclement weather. The gardens were lost, the maze of brick pathways broken and forgotten. The whole place wore an air of despair and long-buried secrets.

Those secrets and the steamy humidity stole Detective Adaline Kinsella's breath as she ducked under the crime-scene tape and pushed open the front door. It swung inward with the inevitable squeak, drawing a shiver.

She had the strangest sensation of déjà vu as she entered the house, and the experience both puzzled and unsettled her. She'd never been here before. Couldn't remember ever having driven down this street. But a nerve had been touched. Old memories had been triggered. If she listened closely enough, she could hear the echo of long-dead screams, but she knew that sound came straight from her nightmares.

She was just tired, Addie told herself. Five days of hiking, swimming and kayaking in ninety-degree weather had taken a toll, and now she needed a vacation from her vacation.

For nearly a week, she'd remained sequestered in her aunt's lake house without access to cable or the internet. One day had spun into another, and for the better part of the week, Addie had thought she'd found heaven on earth in the Blue Ridge Mountains. But by Thursday she'd become restless to the point of pacing on the front porch. On Friday she'd awakened early, packed up her car and headed back to Charleston, arriving just after lunch to explosive headlines and the police department abuzz with a gruesome discovery.

The details of that find swirled in her head as she hovered in the foyer. The previous owner of the house, a recluse named Delmar Gainey, had died five years earlier in a nursing home, and the property had remained vacant until an enterprising house flipper had bought it at auction. The demo crew had noticed a fusty odor, but no one had sounded an alarm. It was the smell of old death, after all. The lingering aroma of disintegrating vermin and rotting vegetation. The house had flooded at least once, allowing in the deadly invasion of mold and mildew. The structure was a public health hazard that needed to be razed, but the flipper had been adamant about renovation—

until his workers had uncovered human remains behind the living room walls.

Skeletal remains had also been found behind the dining room walls and beneath the rotting floorboards in the hallway. Seven bodies hidden away inside the abandoned house and seven more buried in the backyard. Fourteen victims so far, and the search had now been extended onto the adjacent property.

"Hello?" Addie called as she moved across the foyer to the rickety staircase. The house was oppressive and sweltering. No power meant no lights and no AC. Sweat trickled down her backbone and moistened her armpits. Furtive claws scratched overhead, and the sound deepened Addie's dread. Ever since she'd heard about the Gainey house, images had bombarded her. Now she pictured the ceiling collapsing and rat bodies dropping down on her. She had a thing about rats. Spiders and snakes she could handle, but rats...

Grimacing in disgust, she moved toward the archway on her right, peeking into the shadowy space she thought might once have been the dining room. The long windows were boarded up, allowing only thin slivers of light to creep in. She could smell dust from the demolished plaster and a whiff of putrefaction. Or was that, too, her imagination? Delmar Gainey's victims had been entombed in the walls for over two decades. Surely the scent would have disintegrated by now.

A memory flitted and was gone. The night-mares still tugged…

Addie suppressed another shiver and wondered why she had come. As of Monday, she had a new assignment. Handpicked by her captain to train with the FBI's famous Behavioral Analysis Unit, she'd been temporarily reassigned from the Charleston PD Investigations Bureau. Soon she would join select law enforcement personnel from all over the Southeast for six weeks of specialized training conducted by one of the brightest minds to ever work in the BAU. But for today, right this moment, she needed to focus on her perilous surroundings. She needed to find out why so many alarms were tripping inside her head.

"Boo!" a voice boomed from the shadows.

Addie jumped in spite of herself, and her hand went automatically to her weapon. Then she let loose a string of expletives that seemed to echo back to her from the hollowed-out walls. "Are you crazy?" she scolded her partner. "I might have shot you."

Detective Matt Lepear laughed as he emerged from the depths of the gloom. "Oh, come on," he drawled. "I've never known anyone less trigger-happy than you." He somehow made it sound like a shortcoming.

"Maybe I've changed."

"Not you, Addie Kinsella. You're as predictable as the day is long. I knew you wouldn't make it a week in the mountains all by your lonesome. What happened? Couldn't stand your own company?"

"Figured I'd better head on back and see how badly you've screwed things up in my absence."

"Can't say as I've missed that mouth." He shoved his dust mask to the top of his head, allowing a lock of brown hair to fall across his brow. "Seriously, girl, you couldn't find anything better to do with the last few days of your vacation? Go to the movies or something. Go shopping, get your hair done. Just go. Get out of here. We've got this covered."

"I know you do, but I wanted to see this place for myself."

"You're a strange bird, Addie. Anyone ever tell you that?"

"Yes, you. All the time."

He leaned a shoulder against the door frame and unwrapped a stick of gum. Like Addie, Matt Lepear was a ten-year veteran of the Charleston PD. They'd gone through the academy together, patrolled the streets together, and their partnership in the Investigations Bureau had seemed a natural progression of their bond. They were as thick as thieves and as different as night and day. Addie had a tendency to overthink and second-guess, but nothing much fazed Matt Lepear. He took it all in stride. Serial killers, hurricanes, even his two ex-wives.

He was a good detective, one might even say gifted, but his career would always be held back by his disdain for rules and neckties. He preferred to follow his gut rather than the book, and he insisted on dressing in his own uniform of jeans, sneakers and T-shirts. His insubordination had become legendary, but he and Addie led the department in percentage of closed cases, so the powers that be tended to give him leeway. Addie was under no illusion that she would be afforded the same consideration with a different partner, no matter that the deputy chief was a man she once called uncle. Addie was smart, meticulous and persistent to a fault, but she would never have Matt's instincts.

His irreverence had rubbed off on her over the years and now she was in no position to criticize anyone's style, she acknowledged, wiping clammy hands down the sides of her faded jeans. She hadn't bothered going home to change before stopping by headquarters. When she heard about the Gainey house, she'd driven straight over. Come Monday, she'd make more of an effort to look presentable. It was in her best interests to get off on the right foot with the retired supervisory special agent-turned-consultant who would be in charge of her training. If there was anything Gwen Holloway had been known for at Quantico, besides her uncanny profiles, it was her rigid standards on dress and conduct.

"You want the twenty-five-cent tour?" Matt asked her.

"Of the house? No, thanks. I'll just poke around on my own." She turned back to the foyer. "How do you think he got away with it for so long? The stench must have been unbearable, especially in the summer months. Yet none of the neighbors ever filed a complaint? Even now I can smell the decay."

"You're smelling the rats," Matt said. "This place is lousy with them, dead and alive."

Addie lifted her gaze to the water-stained ceiling. "I can hear them."

"Wait until they start nipping at your feet. As to why the neighbors never complained, you have to remember that back in Delmar Gainey's time, this area was a lot less populated. The houses damaged by the hurricane were either torn down or abandoned. Gainey's mother died the same year the big one hit. He moved in after she passed, and that's likely when he began his spree. Her death may even have been the stressor. Being isolated as he was, he could come and go as he pleased— bury bodies in the backyard at all hours—and no one would have noticed."

"And then he just stopped?"

Matt nodded toward the murky sidelights that flanked the front door. "Didn't you notice the ramp by the porch steps? Three years after Gainey moved in here, he had a car accident that confined him to a wheelchair. His mobility became limited. He couldn't go around unnoticed like he did before the accident, so for the next quarter of a century, he had to content himself with reliving the kills in his head. Probably why he stayed in this squalor for as long as did. Couldn't bear leaving his conquests behind."

Addie glanced around the gutted room. The remains had already been removed and the scene processed, but the exposed wall studs were a reminder of a madman's gruesome pastime. "That explains how the smell went unnoticed, but how do fourteen people in a city this size just disappear?"

"Fringe dwellers, most likely. Street people have always been easy prey. We'll have to check the files to see if any of the disappearances were reported. That far back, nothing is computerized. Someone will have to do some digging."

Addie nodded absently, her gaze still raking over the walls.

"There's also the time frame to consider." Matt's voice sounded hushed, as if he had intuited her unease. "Could be the reason the disappearances never made the news is because Gainey's spree overlapped with a more famous predator."

Addie nodded again, but she found herself oddly short of breath. Why Matt's observation should hit her so hard, she couldn't explain. She'd already considered the timeline, but the spoken word had power. In one sentence, her partner had illuminated a connection, no matter how tenuous and indirect, to Addie's personal nightmare. The déjà vu she'd experienced upon arrival hadn't been conjured by this house, but by the icy touch of another monster.

"Think about everything going on in Charleston during that time," Matt said. "The city knee-deep in hurricane recovery and every headline and news broadcast obsessed with the Twilight Killer."

The Twilight Killer. The very real bogeyman of Addie's childhood.

"Little wonder someone like Gainey was able to fly under the radar."

"I guess." Addie turned to avoid her partner's penetrating gaze.

His voice softened. "You still don't like to talk about it, do you?"

"I don't mind talking about it. I just have nothing new to offer. And it happened so long ago. I barely even remember it." Not true, of course. She recalled only too well the woman she called aunt standing in the bedroom doorway as Addie had pretended to sleep.

How do we do this, David? That child is barely seven years old. How do we explain to someone so young that her mother has been brutally murdered by a serial killer? Only, it couldn't have been Orson Lee Finch, could it? You arrested him. Which means there's another one out there. A copycat...

We're not going to explain anything tonight. The news can wait until morning. Come away from the door, Helen. Let the girl sleep.

In a minute. I just can't bear to take my eyes off her. My poor angel...

Orson Lee Finch's spree had lasted five months. Nine young women had been brutally murdered, all single mothers from affluent families. All slain in the twilight hour by a demented gardener who had left as his calling card a crimson magnolia petal placed on the lips of his victims, as if to seal their deaths with a kiss.

Unlike Delmar Gainey, who had sequestered his victims in his home, Orson Lee Finch had flaunted his kills, leaving the bodies broken and exposed.

Addie's mother had been the ninth victim— or the first, depending on one's perspective. She hadn't been killed by Orson Lee Finch, but her death was a result of his spree. She'd been murdered in cold blood by the FBI profiler who had mind-hunted Finch. For months, SSA James Merrick had tireless tracked the Twilight Killer, only to become the monster he had so obsessively stalked.

"I watched a documentary the other night about the Twilight Killer," Matt said. "They interviewed people who still think Orson Lee Finch is innocent."

"Death-row groupies. I've run into a few of those over the years," Addie said.

"No, these people were different. Articulate and respectful, and they made some good points. Got me to thinking."

"Had to happen sooner or later."

Matt grinned and folded his arms, which meant he had no intention of letting the subject drop until he'd said his piece. "The case had inconsistencies that I was unaware of until I saw that film. They also ran a segment on Twilight's Children." He paused. "They showed your picture, but it didn't look much like you."

"Probably an old shot," Addie said, still avoiding his gaze.

"They said you declined to be interviewed."

"Because I'm not technically one of Twilight's Children. Orson Lee Finch didn't kill my mother."

"Yeah, but they lump you in just the same, and they still consider your mother the ninth victim. You have to admit, it was one strange, messed-up case."

"*Messed up* is an understatement," Addie muttered.

Matt continued, undaunted, "An FBI profiler with an almost godlike reputation helps capture the psycho and then ends up stalking and murdering a victim with the same MO in order to continue Finch's mission. Talk about crazy."

"Merrick obviously had a psychotic breakdown," Addie said. "Which is why he remains to this day in the state psychiatric hospital in Columbia. He's where he belongs. End of story. Let's get back to Delmar Gainey. We're standing in his house of horrors, after all."

"Yeah, sure. We can get back to Gainey. But there's a lesson to be learned from James Merrick. Especially for you."

She frowned. "What are you talking about?"

"Your new assignment." He let his head fall back against the door frame as he observed her. "It's a game changer. I'd be the last one to ever stand in your way."

"I know that. I also know you deserve this assignment more than I do."

"That's not true. You're a good detective, and you're smart. You need to stop selling yourself short because of a stupid rookie mistake."

Addie winced.

"Just stay smart, okay? The people who'll be training you are a different breed. Next-level intense. What we found here is nothing compared to what they deal with on a daily basis."

"What's your point?"

"Sooner or later, what they do takes a toll. It has to if you're human."

"You don't think I can handle it?"

"Oh, I know you can handle it. Just be aware. Profiling is a powerful tool, but it's not without a dark side. It can mess with your head if you're not careful."

"You mean like James Merrick."

"He entered the mind of a monster and created an opening, allowing the monster to slither back into his." Matt's gaze deepened, and he seemed uncharacteristically sober. "You go into that training with an open mind, Addie. Learn everything you can from this Gwen Holloway. Be a sponge. Soak it all up. Then you come back to the Charleston PD and put that knowledge to good use. But always keep your guard up. Always protect yourself. The moment you let that monster crawl inside your head and make a nest is the moment you become the next James Merrick."

SPECIAL AGENT ETHAN BARROW stood at rigid attention beside his rented SUV as he eyed the abandoned house through his Ray-Bans. His gaze traveled over the crumbling roofline and then dropped once more to the sagging porch. The place was as dark and creepy as one might imagine the lair of a ruthless predator would be. Even the sun shining down through thick curtains of Spanish moss seemed muted, casting the house in perpetual gloom.

Ever since Ethan's return to Charleston, the news had been dominated by the gruesome discovery inside that house, managing to over-shadow the upcoming anniversary of Orson Lee Finch's incarceration and James Merrick's subsequent confinement to the state psychiatric hospital. Twenty-five years after the fact, Orson Lee Finch remained at Kirkland Correctional Institution, housed in a specialized unit for the state's most violent inmates. Most people thought he deserved worse. James Merrick remained a patient on the infamous fourth floor, a ward for the criminally insane. Most people thought he deserved worse.

Ethan wasn't one of those people.

He shifted his position so that he could glimpse around the corner of the house. He heard voices over the fence, but no one approached him. That was good. He needed a few minutes to plot his strategy. Or to work up his courage. No reason in the world Adaline Kinsella should agree to hear him out after what he'd once put her through, but she was the only person he could turn to right now. The only person he trusted with the potential bombshell that had fallen into his lap.

He moved back to the other end of the SUV, killing more time. It had now been twenty-four hours since his arrival in Charleston, and he had yet to make contact with Addie. He hadn't slept much. He'd eaten poorly, consumed too much coffee, and now he was starting to feel the strain. He'd forgotten just how hot and humid the city could be in the middle of summer. Virginia was bad enough, but coastal South Carolina was a whole new level of misery. He wasn't dressed for the weather. He loosened his tie and tugged at the collar of his starched shirt, but he didn't remove his jacket. The dark suit was his uniform now. Both his identity and his camouflage.

His first order of business upon landing at Charleston International Airport the day before had been to rent a vehicle and drive to Columbia to interview Orson Lee Finch. Over the years, Ethan had studied dozens, perhaps hundreds, of photos and videos of Finch, but he'd never met him in person. Face-to-face, Finch's appearance had taken him by surprise. The Twilight Killer was a small man, pale and wiry with bright blue eyes magnified behind the thick lenses of silver-framed glasses. His grooming was fastidious—crisp khaki uniform, combed hair, clean and clipped nails. He resembled a scholar or historian. He did not look like a serial killer. Ethan couldn't help but wonder how Finch had managed to survive for as long as he had behind bars. Maybe he was small enough and his appearance so nondescript that he'd managed to go unnoticed. Or maybe his looks were deceiving.

They'd sat on plastic chairs, eyeing each other warily through the partition until Finch had picked up the phone. A few minutes of awkward conversation had ensued while Ethan tried to get a feel for his subject. Finch had struck him as quiet and reflective, a man who'd long ago made peace with his deeds and circumstances. His placid demeanor never altered until Ethan had broached the topic of Finch's mother. Then the blue eyes seemed to intensify behind the glasses and the corner of Finch's mouth twitched, as if he were suppressing a painful memory.

"Your mother never married, did she?" Ethan had spoken in a conversational tone, trying to draw the man out. "That must have been tough. Children born out of wedlock were stigmatized back in your day. You were probably teased in school, maybe even bullied."

Finch said nothing.

"Your mother worked as a housekeeper, so I imagine money was tight. Barely enough for necessities, let alone extras. You wore hand-me-down clothing from the people whose houses she cleaned, and as much as you enjoyed having those nice things, you resented where they came from, didn't you? You were hostile to the hand that fed you."

Finch watched him avidly through the partition.

Ethan glanced down at his notes even though he had everything memorized. "Despite your disadvantages, you were a good student. Always the brightest in your class, but your financial situation limited your prospects. A full-ride scholarship must have been the answer to all your prayers. A dream come true. You studied horticulture at a state school, right? You wanted to be a landscape architect. Then your mother became ill during your junior year, and you were forced to drop out of college to take care of her. That's when you got your first job as a gardener. You had to go back, hat in hand, to the people who had given you their throwaway clothing."

Finch had stared at him for the longest moment before answering. "Is this your way of establishing rapport, Special Agent Barrow? Or do you wish to impress me with the amount of homework you've done?"

"How's this for homework? You have a daughter out there somewhere. No one knows her name or where she's been since your incarceration. Some believe her mother was your first victim. Did she fit your criteria? A single mother without morals. A loose woman who valued her freedom more than her child. What happened? Did she refuse to marry you? Is that what set you off?"

Finch's expression never changed, but something dark glinted at the back of his eyes. "After all these years and all the files you people have amassed—mountains, I'm told—no one has ever gotten it right. Not even the esteemed James Merrick."

"Is that a denial?"

Finch studied his hand for a moment. "Merrick's profile was flawed from the start. It was written from the cynical presumption that I harbored ill will toward my own mother. Nothing could be further from the truth. I was a happy child. We didn't have money, but I never wanted for affection. I wasn't starved for attention. Your psychological evaluations to the contrary, I wasn't bitter then about my lot in life and I'm not bitter now. That must surprise you. You're thinking, if he's really innocent, how can he be so accepting of such a cruel injustice?"

"How do you accept it? If you really are innocent, that is."

A smile flickered for the first time. "I could never give an explanation that would satisfy someone like you. Acceptance isn't in your nature. A man like you will always be at war with his emotions. Tormented by what he can't know. Unable to make peace with his past."

Damn if the observation hadn't been insightful and perhaps even prophetic.

After Ethan had left Orson Lee Finch, he'd driven to the state psychiatric hospital. He was no stranger to the layout of the parking area or the maze of hallways and wards. He'd visited regularly for years and was afforded certain privileges because of his position and background. He had signed in and then been escorted up to the fourth floor, where an orderly had unlocked a small room and waved Ethan inside.

James Merrick had been at the window, gazing out over the shady grounds. He hadn't turned when Ethan entered, nor had he acknowledged Ethan's presence in any way. That wasn't unusual. He never gave any indication of recognizing Ethan from one visit to the next. Ethan had learned to ignore the long silences and unblinking stares, as well as the disturbing sounds that came from deep within the facility. He focused his attention instead on the patient's journals, poring over pages and pages of painstakingly scribbled gibberish in the hope of finding the one clue that would break everything open.

He had that clue now. The last piece of the puzzle was finally within his grasp.

"I came here to tell you that new evidence has turned up in your case," he'd said to Merrick.

The man had given no indication of comprehension, but Ethan hadn't let the prolonged silence discourage him.

"I won't go into the details yet. It's early stages of the investigation. But I wanted you to know that I'm still out there looking for the truth. I never believed you were guilty. Not once in all these years." Ethan walked over to the window and placed his hand briefly on the man's frail arm. "Do you remember me?" he murmured. "I'm Ethan."

Nothing so much as a blink.

"I work for the FBI just as you did. I even do

support investigations for the BAU. Back in your day, it was called the Behavioral Science Unit."

Still no response.

"My stepfather is Richard Barrow. You knew him once. I took his name when he married my mother, but he's not my dad. My real name is Merrick. Ethan Merrick. I'm your son."

Chapter Two

The muted thrum of a car engine drew Ethan's attention, pulling him out of that twelve-by-twelve room, away from the power of his father's vacant stare and back to his roadside vigil in front of the Gainey house.

He turned his head toward the sound, noting the presence of a black Dodge Charger—the preferred FBI pursuit vehicle—at the end of the street. The car did not approach, nor did the driver pull to the curb to accommodate oncoming traffic. The Charger sat idling in the middle of the road as if daring Ethan to notice.

Any hope he'd had of flying under the radar vanished. He'd seen that same vehicle or one like it parked outside his hotel that morning. Ethan had gone about his business, taking tortuous routes as he ran aimless errands, and eventually he'd lost the tail in downtown traffic. He had no doubt, though, that whoever was keeping tabs on him had already heard about his trip to Columbia and his visit that morning to the Charleston Police

Department. He supposed he shouldn't be surprised that they'd found him again so quickly—they were pros, after all—but it had only been by sheer luck that he'd overheard mention of Adaline Kinsella's name and her whereabouts. He had no idea why the agents had thought to look for him here unless they'd known all along he would come to Addie.

He glanced around, once again scoping out his surroundings. He needed an exit strategy in case the occupants of the Charger got too curious. The house sat at the end of a dead-end street, nearly hidden by a canopy of live oaks and palm trees. The nearest neighbor was a block away, but Ethan was hardly alone. While he stood contemplating his options, the voices behind the fence grew louder, and through one of the grimy sidelights, he caught the silhouette of a woman.

Was it Addie?

Had she spotted him?

Probably not, he decided. If she had an inkling of his presence, she would have already come outside to give him a piece of her mind. Not that he could blame her. He deserved every insult and condemnation she could heap upon him. Still, he'd come here with *his* hat in hand, offering her the chance to help solve the case of a lifetime.

He squinted down the end of the road, trying to determine if the car had crept a little closer. Even from a distance, he could tell the windows were tinted and the license plate obscured. He wondered briefly if a tracker had been planted on his vehicle. Maybe that was how they'd found him again so quickly. More likely they'd used his phone's GPS. Electronic surveillance usually meant clout and someone with serious intent.

The surveillance had annoyed him earlier, but now he was just plain pissed. He resented having his every move scrutinized and disseminated. He'd used personal days to come to Charleston on his own dime, relying on his own resources. As far as he was concerned, this was not the FBI's business, but of course, his section chief would likely see things differently.

So be it. Might as well give them enough rope.

He climbed into his rental and made a U-turn in the street, picking up speed as he headed toward the Charger. The acceleration thrilled him. He pushed the pedal to the floor, and the powerful V-8 roared. The scenery blurred in the side windows as the vehicle shot forward.

For a moment, he wondered if the driver meant to call his bluff. The vehicle remained immobile for so long that a crash seemed imminent. Ethan braced himself and was just about to swerve when the car reversed down the street and backed around the corner in one smooth move. Then the driver shifted and the Charger catapulted through the intersection.

Ethan made the turn without slowing. He

gripped the wheel as the SUV fishtailed and the tires spun on the graveled shoulder. Up ahead, the Charger careened around another corner and blasted through a stop sign, narrowly missing a woman and two small boys as they stepped off the curb. The mother had plenty of time to pull the children to safety on the sidewalk, but she froze. Ethan could have sworn he saw her lips move in prayer a split second before he hit the brakes.

The tires squealed in protest as the rubber gripped the pavement and the powerful vehicle skidded to a stop.

He hopped out of the SUV and called to the woman, "Are you okay?"

She spoke in a heavy accent. "Are you crazy? You could have killed us!"

She kept screaming at him, gesturing wildly with her arms as the boys clung to her legs. Ethan stood silently by and took it. She had every right to call him out. What had he been thinking, engaging in a high-speed chase?

He scanned the neighborhood from his periphery. Many of the houses along the street were in various stages of disrepair, but he could see signs of gentrification creeping in. He wondered what the upwardly mobile millennials would think of their fixer-upper investments when they learned about the house at the end of the dead-end street.

Apologizing profusely, he got back in his vehicle. He waited until the woman was safely across the street with the children and then he circled the block and headed back to the abandoned house, parking in the very spot he had vacated only a few minutes earlier. The incident left him shaken. He'd been able to stop in plenty of time, but that was beside the point. What if his brakes had failed? What if he'd lost control of the wheel? He'd behaved recklessly, and that wasn't like him. Not anymore. Maybe he'd played the game for too long, kept his head down and his nose clean for so long that his dangerous impulses were rebelling. Ever since he'd received the first email from a woman named Naomi Quinlan, his life had been one risky decision after another.

He locked the vehicle and walked through the tall weeds in the front yard, pausing at the bottom of the steps to scan the ramshackle facade. He could no longer see anyone inside. Whoever he'd glimpsed earlier had moved into another part of the house or perhaps had left the premises altogether. He hoped that wasn't the case. Far better that he approach Addie on neutral ground than to show up unexpectedly at her house.

He lifted the crime-scene tape over his head and opened the front door. Before he could step into the foyer, a male voice halted him. "Stop right there. In case you can't read that yellow tape, this is a crime scene. You need to get back behind the barricade and stay there."

Ethan took out his wallet and showed the man

his credentials. "My name is Ethan Barrow. I'm with the FBI."

The man glanced at the badge and scowled. "No one said anything about federal involvement."

Ethan returned the wallet to his pocket and removed his sunglasses. "I didn't catch your name."

"Detective Matthew Lepear, Charleston PD." He glanced behind him into the gutted room. "Delmar Gainey's victims have been dead for over two decades, Agent Barrow. The man himself died five years ago. Why would the feds be interested in this case?"

"I'm not interested in your case, Detective. I'm looking for Adaline Kinsella."

"What's your interest in *Detective* Kinsella, if you don't mind my asking?"

The slight proprietorial edge in the man's voice caught Ethan's attention. He gave him a sharper scrutiny. "I'd rather discuss my business with her."

"Detective Kinsella is on vacation this week."

Ethan turned to glance out one of the sidelights before resettling his gaze on the detective. "Isn't that her silver SUV at the curb?"

The man shrugged. "New cars all look alike."

Ethan folded his sunglasses carefully and tucked them into his inner jacket pocket. "Detective Kinsella is your partner, isn't she?"

"Why do you ask?"

"You seem overly protective. I can appreciate your concern, but I'm not sure she would."

Something flashed in Lepear's eyes, a fleeting acknowledgment that Ethan had hit a little too close to the truth. "You could be right. Addie's got a mind of her own, that's for damn sure. The one thing I do know about her is this—she won't be happy to see you."

Ethan tamped down his annoyance. "You know her well enough to make that assessment?"

"We go back a long way. Ten years, to be precise. She's not just my partner. She's also a friend. And you're the SOB who almost ended her career."

Ethan was jolted by an uncomfortable truth. Lepear knew who he was.

Anger mingled with remorse. "I never meant to cause her trouble."

"People like you never do. You just tell yourself the end justifies the means."

Ethan waited a beat before he continued. He didn't want to lose his temper. Lepear was defending his partner and friend. Ethan would do the same if the positions were reversed, but it wasn't like he'd walked away from the relationship unscathed. It wasn't like he'd gone back to Virginia and forgotten all about Adaline Kinsella. He'd spent many a sleepless night staring up at the ceiling, wanting to call just to hear her voice but knowing she would never pick up.

"I'm not looking for trouble now," he said. "I just want to talk to her."

Lepear gave him a derisive look before he finally acquiesced. "She's out back. You can go through that door." He nodded toward the crumbling archway. "But if I were you, I'd watch my step. I mean, I'd *really* watch my step, Agent Barrow."

Their gazes held for a moment longer before Ethan nodded. "Thanks for the heads-up."

ADDIE STOOD ON the back porch, staring at the mounds of dirt and empty graves where the remains had been excavated and removed. A broken wheelchair had been pushed up under the porch railing, and she couldn't help but imagine Delmar Gainey sitting there alone in the dark, admiring his gruesome garden by moonlight. Another ramp had been built beside the back steps, and if Addie closed her eyes, she could see him out there among the graves, enjoying the mingled scents of jasmine and death wafting on the afternoon breeze.

She felt light-headed from the heat and from old memories, and she curled her fingers around the wood rail, clinging for a moment while she tried to beat back her emotions. She was no stranger to death. She'd lost her mother to a brutal killer and her grandmother to the gentler reaper of natural causes. As a cop, Addie had seen all manner of death and violence, but those empty graves reminded her of the thin veneer of humanity that could too easily be peeled away.

A sound brought her around with a start, and she felt a shudder go through her as her gaze connected with the man in the doorway. Tall and fit, he stood ramrod straight in his dark suit and tie, hardly more than a silhouette against the dim backdrop of the house.

"Ethan?" Even as she spoke his name, her chin came up in defiance. Before she could demand to know the purpose of his presence, she heard a crack, followed by a splintering sound as the rotting floorboards gave way beneath her feet. Her arms flailed wildly as she tried to catch her balance, but the wood disintegrated and she crashed through the porch.

She saw Ethan lunge for her, and then she saw nothing but blackness as she found herself in a free fall.

Chapter Three

Addie reached out instinctively, grasping, grasping until she made contact with a rope. She grabbed on with both hands, halting her fall for only an instant before she dropped to the bottom. But that split second allowed her to brace for impact. She tucked and rolled.

Hot pain shot across her left shoulder as she lay still for a moment. Then she gingerly moved her arms and legs. No broken bones. She pushed herself off the floor and got to her feet. No cuts or other wounds that she could determine, but she was in complete darkness save for a thin tunnel of illumination that shone down through the fractured boards. The light seemed to quiver as if it had a life of its own. The sensation was eerie and disorienting. Addie reached out with one hand and made contact with the wall as she tilted her head to that shimmering light.

"Addie?"

Her eyes fluttered closed before she braced herself yet again. That voice. How many times had she dreamed of it in her ear, imagined his husky whisper in the dark? She shivered now as her name echoed off the walls like a taunt.

"Adaline, can you hear me?"

She peered up into the freaky light. "I can hear you."

"Are you okay?"

"I'm okay. No broken bones or cuts. Where am I?"

"I think you've fallen into an old well or cistern. The porch must have been built over it. Are you in water?"

She shivered again at the echo-like quality of his voice. "No, but the walls are damp. And it smells pretty bad down here. I wonder how far I fell. It looks a long way up there."

"Hard to say. Fifteen, twenty feet maybe. You're lucky you didn't break your neck."

"I grabbed on to a rope. Do you see it?"

"It looks badly frayed. I'm not sure it's strong enough to haul you up."

"Go find Matt. Matt Lepear. He's my partner. He drove his truck out here today. He usually keeps a chain in the back for when he goes off-roading. Someone always gets stuck."

"I'll find him and we'll get you out of there. Just hang tight until I get back."

"Ethan?"

His face appeared back over the opening.

"Someone left a flashlight on the porch railing.

I saw it a minute ago. Can you toss it down to me? It's pitch-black and I think I hear rats."

"I see it. I'll tie it off and lower it down. Stand back in case the rope breaks."

She stepped out of the light, allowing the darkness to swallow her. Furtive claws scratched nearby, and she could have sworn something scurried across her feet, but she hoped the sensation wasn't real. She hoped her imagination was getting the better of her because the notion of rats closing in on her—

Ethan cut into her thoughts. "I'm lowering the light down now."

He turned on the bulb so that Addie could track the beam. As the rope spun, the light bounced off the walls, casting giant shadows down into the well. Addie reached eagerly for the flashlight, slipping it free of the knot and then wrapping her fingers tightly around the thick rubber housing.

"I've got it," she said. "Thanks."

"No problem. I'll be right back."

"Ethan?"

"Yes?"

She ran the light up and down the walls and then over the floor, exploring debris that had been abandoned for decades.

"What is it?" he called down to her.

"There's a lot of trash in here." Her voice quivered in spite of her best efforts. "Old blankets. Broken dishes. I think this is where he kept them."

Ethan said something, but she didn't hear his response. She was too caught up in the horror of that place. Too distracted by the image of that wheelchair shoved up under the porch railing. How many times had Gainey rolled across the floorboards, aroused by his memories as he reveled in his secrets?

Addie angled the beam along the crevice where floor met wall. She imagined someone cowering there, but the beady eyes that glinted back at her weren't human.

Repelled by the light, the rat scuttled back to its hidey-hole, leaving Addie alone with the echo of long-dead screams.

ADDIE STOOD WITH her face to the sun, basking in the light as she brushed dust from her hair. Even covered in dirt and grime, she looked good. Ethan was glad for his sunglasses so he could pretend not to stare.

He and some of the officers had easily hauled her up from the well, and she seemed no worse for the wear. But she hadn't lingered, even when her partner had insisted on going down to have a look for himself. Addie had watched for a moment and then, with a shudder, turned and disappeared. Ethan had followed her out into the sun. After the creepy confines of that house, he welcomed the heat, even the trickle of sweat he could feel between his shoulder blades.

"You okay?" he asked.

"I just needed some air. Being down in that well and knowing what he used it for...knowing what he did to all those people...it got to me for a minute."

Ethan nodded. "It gets to all of us now and then, but that's a good thing. You don't ever want to feel numb to what one human being can do to another. You never want to lose your ability to be shocked."

If she thought that sentiment strange coming from him—the son of a profiler who had gone to the dark side—she didn't say so. "You see this sort of thing more than I do. How do you cope?"

"I'd be lying if I said I leave it at the office. But I try to find productive ways to fill up my spare time. I run. I listen to music and read books. Sometimes I visit museums and art galleries just to remind myself that human beings are also capable of creating great beauty."

"That sounds amazingly well adjusted. Right now, I just want a good, stiff drink." She wiped her hands down the sides of her jeans as if trying to cleanse herself of the images.

Ethan found himself checking out her fingers to make sure she hadn't gotten married or engaged since last he'd heard. No diamonds that he could discern, but the sun bouncing off the detective shield she'd clipped to her waist was blinding.

"Congratulations, by the way."

She gave him a suspicious look. "For what?"

He nodded toward her badge. "You made detective in record time, I see."

Her eyes flashed. "I didn't set any records. And there were plenty of times when I never thought I'd make it. This shield didn't just fall into my lap. I worked hard for it."

He'd obviously hit a nerve. Like him, she'd probably battled whispers of nepotism for most of her career. "I never thought otherwise," he said. "My congratulations were sincere."

"Thank you." She glanced away for a moment as if trying to puzzle something out. Her gaze came back to him reluctantly. "You seem different."

"Because I'm happy for your success?"

A frown flitted across her brow. "No. I can't put my finger on it."

"It's been ten years. I expect we're both different people."

"Agreed. At the very least, I like to think I'm a lot less gullible than I used to be."

Their gazes met, clashed again, but behind the glimmer of hostility, Ethan felt a connection, no matter how fleeting. Or maybe the link was nothing more than wishful thinking, but he found himself drifting back, imagining her smile and the spill of blond hair over her shoulders as she stared down at him through hooded eyes. Adaline Kinsella at twenty-two had been something. At thirty-two… Ethan didn't dare let himself go there.

She glanced past him down the road to where the black Charger had returned to wait him out. "Friends of yours?"

"No."

She lifted a brow at his tone. "Enemies?"

"I don't know."

"But they're here because of you."

"Probably."

"That car looks official. Tinted windows. No identifying tags or marks. I'm guessing feds." Her gaze swung back to him. "Why are *you* here, Ethan? What have you done this time?"

"You don't pull any punches, do you?"

Any hint of a bond melted in the fierceness of her stare. "I've been on the wrong end of your obsession, remember? I recognize the signs. You didn't come all the way from Quantico just to see me."

"Why not? It wouldn't be the first time."

"Okay, stop right there." She gave him a disgusted look. "Don't even think about playing that card. In case you've forgotten, things didn't end well for us. So don't pretend this is a sentimental reunion. Be honest for once in your life and tell me why you're really here."

"It's not an easy explanation."

"It never is with you." She came down the

porch steps. "How did you even know where to find me, anyway? I've been away on vacation. I only got back a little while ago, and other than a quick stop at the station, I came straight here." She shot another glance at the Charger. "If those guys are following *me*—"

"They're not. Stop worrying about that car. I'll handle whoever's inside. I knew to find you at this house because I overheard someone at police headquarters mention your whereabouts."

The revelation didn't please her. "You were at headquarters? Who did you talk to?"

"I didn't talk to anyone about you. I had a meeting with the deputy chief."

She looked even more distressed. "Why?"

"That's for him to say."

Addie shook her head. "This is crazy. I don't want to hear any more. Whatever you're involved in, count me out. Thanks for getting me out of the well. I do appreciate that. But this is the end of the road for us." She turned and headed for her vehicle. "I'm going home and you can go to…" Down the road, a car door slammed, freezing her for a moment as she glanced over her shoulder.

One of the agents had gotten out of the Charger to stretch, apparently now unconcerned about anonymity. Ethan didn't recognize him, but like Addie, he knew the guy was a federal agent.

He returned his focus to Addie. She lifted her

chin and turned back to her car. He called after her. "I've found new evidence in your mother's case."

That stopped her again. She turned slowly to face him. "What?"

"I wasn't lying when I said I came to Charleston to see you, but I'm also here pursuing a lead. I wanted you to know before you heard it from someone else."

"Is that why you went to see the deputy chief?"

"Like I said, you need to talk to him about that."

She shoved back a lock of damp hair. "Assuming I believe you, what makes you think I'd ever want any of this dumped on my doorstep?"

"Besides the fact that your mother was murdered? You're a police detective. You must be interested in justice."

She said nothing for the longest time, just stood there staring back at him as he searched her face. Her eyes were so much bluer than he remembered. Softer, too, and liquid. They reminded him of a Monet painting he'd seen in the National Gallery.

But right now, those eyes were narrowed in suspicion. "My mother's case is closed. As far as I'm concerned, justice was served twenty-five years ago when your father was committed to the fourth floor."

"Maybe. Or maybe an innocent man was framed for something he didn't do."

"James Merrick is not an innocent man." She opened her car door. "I've heard enough. I'm not getting sucked back into your delusions. Listening to you almost cost me everything ten years ago."

"If the evidence wasn't compelling, I wouldn't be here."

"Then investigate all you want, but leave me out of it."

"Addie."

She whirled. "Damn it, can't you take a hint? Leave me alone!"

Her tone took him aback. He put up a hand. "Okay. I get it. I'm sorry I bothered you."

She let out a long sigh. "Don't give me that look. Do you think I enjoy acting like a first-class bitch?"

"I would never call you that."

"You didn't have to. I can hear myself. I don't enjoy saying these things to you, Ethan. I'm not an angry person, and I don't like carrying a grudge. But you did lie to me. And worse, you got *me* to lie. That was on me. As a grown woman, I should have known better. I never should have accessed sealed files without authorization, let alone allowed you to leak information to the press. I shouldn't have done a lot of things I did when I was with you, but that all happened a long time ago. I'm over it. What I can't get past, though, is how you made me doubt myself. How you made me lose faith that I had what it took to be a good cop. I've worked really hard to get my confidence back."

No wonder she was so defensive of her detective's shield. "I'm sorry I lied to you. And I'm sorry about how everything went down."

"I know. That I believe, but it doesn't change anything."

"If you'd just hear me out—"

"I can't."

"Five minutes. That's all I'm asking."

She closed her eyes. "Why are you doing this to me?"

"Because you're the only other person in the world I trust with this information. If anything were to happen to me, I know you'd do the right thing."

Her eyes widened. "What do you mean, if anything were to happen to you?"

He shrugged. "We live in a dangerous world."

Her gaze flicked back to the Charger. "Who are those guys?"

"I don't know."

"They're watching you because of this new information?"

"That would be my guess."

She chewed her bottom lip as she stared down the road at the car. "I can't believe I'm saying this, but fine. Tell me what you've found."

He followed her gaze to the Charger. "I'd rather

discuss it somewhere more private. Can I buy you that drink?"

"No," she said bluntly. "When I leave here, I'm going straight home to wash the cobwebs out of my hair."

"Later then. We can meet anywhere you like."

She drew another breath. "I know I'll live to regret this, but I sometimes go for walks on the Battery in the evenings. I'll be there at seven, and I'll wait exactly five minutes. If you don't show, we'll let this drop and you won't ever bother me again."

"Agreed," he said. "But I'll be there."

Nothing short of the apocalypse—or the federal agents inside that black Dodge Charger—could keep him away.

Chapter Four

Addie's house was a modest brick ranch tucked back from the street and shaded by two large live oaks that canopied her whole front yard. Beds of impatiens lined her brick walkway, and hydrangeas grew along the sides of her concrete porch. It was a pleasant place to come home to, a cool and colorful oasis.

Once upon a time, as she'd sanded and refinished the original hardwood floors and painted every wall in the house, she'd had visions of dinner parties and backyard barbecues. But a strange thing happened when she finished her renovations. She became greedy of her privacy and protective of her sanctuary. Most evenings, she was all too content to sit alone in the yard watching hummingbirds fight at her feeders and later, lightning bugs flit through the jasmine.

Today when she turned down her street, she took note of a white panel van parked two doors down from her place. The traditional two-story house was undergoing a gut job, so it wasn't unusual to find any number of vehicles parked at the curb. The side door of the van was open, and Addie glimpsed what looked to be an assortment of tools and lumber inside. The front door to the house was also open, but she saw no signs of life. Addie wasn't alarmed or even that curious; she was merely observant. East Side fixer-uppers had become hot commodities over the past few years, and the heightened activity in the neighborhood sometimes allowed criminals to slip in and out unnoticed. It paid to keep an eye out.

A late-model luxury sedan was parked in her driveway when she got home. This vehicle she recognized. Addie waved to the older woman perched on her porch steps. The woman waved back and called out to her. Just shy of sixty, Dr. Helen Cutler was pleasantly nondescript, neither short nor tall, neither heavy nor thin, but she had an aura of warmth and vitality that drew one in, and her voice was melodic and soothing—desirable attributes for a therapist. She wore her silver hair clipped close to her head, and she favored oversize eyeglasses and knit cotton clothing with a bohemian flare. She sat on the top step with her full skirt flowing around her ankles as she watched Addie cross the yard.

"This is a pleasant surprise. I didn't expect to see you this afternoon," Addie said as she automatically shaded her eyes to check up and down the street. A calico cat rose from the porch, stretched and then sauntered down the steps to greet her at the bottom. She bent to give the feline some attention.

"I didn't expect to see you, either," Helen said. "Not for another two days. As to what *I'm* doing here, did you forget you asked me to feed the strays while you were away?"

"You didn't get my voice mail?"

"I lost my phone," Helen said with a sigh. "Second time this year. One would almost think I'm misplacing them on purpose. Fortunately, my new one arrives tomorrow, although I've rather enjoyed going old-school for the last couple of days."

Addie plopped down on the porch steps beside her. "I'd be lost without my phone."

"Spoken like a true millennial. But David is almost as bad. Sometimes I think he has that thing glued to his ear."

"Your husband is an important man. The department couldn't function without our deputy chief."

"So he tells me," Helen said drily. "But enough about him. Tell me why you're back so early."

Addie pulled her legs up and wrapped her arms around her knees, mimicking Helen's position. The Cutlers weren't blood relatives, but they were closer to Addie than any of her real family. David had been both mentor and taskmaster, and there had been times when Addie had felt he demanded too much of her, that he held her to a higher standard than any of the other detectives. But in the long run, his expectations had served her well, and there was no one in the department she trusted or respected more.

Twenty-five years ago, as a young homicide detective, he'd been the one to find her mother's body. In the painful aftermath of that tragedy, Helen had helped Addie cope with her grief, her night terrors and the confusing notoriety that came from being one of Twilight's Children. The couple had been her lifeline ever since, and Addie knew she would never be able to repay their kindness and support.

"The cabin was wonderful for about three days," she said. "And then I started to go stir-crazy."

Helen glanced at her over the top of her glasses. "With that gorgeous lake right outside your door? All those lovely mountains to explore?"

"What can I say, I'm a city girl at heart. I can only take so much of communing with nature before I need my morning fix of car horns and exhaust fumes."

"You sound just like David. I've been trying to get him to slow down for the past ten years, but he just gets busier and crankier. Sometimes I think he won't be content until he works himself to death. These days he doesn't get home until well after dark, and he leaves the house before I wake up. And lately—" Helen broke off with a frown.

"Lately what?"

"He seems…distant. Distracted. It's probably nothing."

"Have you talked to him about it?"

"You know he doesn't like to talk about work. Not to me, at least."

"Do you want me to talk to him?"

Helen patted her arm. "I would never put you in that position. You might suggest to him, though, that a vacation with his wife wouldn't be the end of the world."

"I'll do that."

"I can't even remember the last time we went up to the cabin together, much less someplace exotic. We used to love taking cruises in our younger days, but the last one must have been before—" She stopped short and then shrugged. "Before he was appointed deputy chief."

"Were you about to say before my mother died?"

Helen was silent for a moment. "How did you know?"

"Because you always get that look when you're thinking about her."

Helen smiled. "You know me too well. Sandra's been on my mind so much lately. This time of year is always difficult, and now with the twenty-fifth anniversary looming, so many articles are coming out about the Twilight Killer and James Merrick. You can't avoid the subject. Or the memories. I was so glad you decided to take your vacation when you did. I wanted you to have some time away from all that darkness."

"Matt Lepear mentioned he saw a documentary about the Twilight Killer the other night," Addie said.

Helen's expression turned grim. "Yes, I saw it, too. I told myself I wouldn't watch, but I couldn't seem to resist."

"He said they showed a picture of me."

"They had photographs of all the children. It was a where-are-they-now montage." She paused, and her voice softened. "So many lives were torn apart that summer. So many children lost their innocence because of that monster. I'm so thankful you've been able to move beyond it."

"In no small part because of you and David," Addie said.

Helen draped an arm around Addie's shoulders and gave her a quick squeeze. "I'm just happy your grandmother allowed us to remain in your life. Your mother and I were always so close. She was like a younger sister to me. And you're the daughter I never had."

Addie tilted her face to the warm breeze. "What was it like that summer? It's all so hazy to me. Like a dream. Yet I can still remember the dress I wore to my mother's funeral and the songs the choir sang. I even remember hearing you and

David talking in the doorway of my bedroom the night she was killed."

Helen glanced at her. "You never told me that."

Addie shrugged. "You always get so sad when we talk about her. I thought it best to keep some things to myself."

Helen regarded her for a moment. "I'm sorry you felt that way. I let you down when you needed me the most."

"That's not true. You *saved* me."

"You saved yourself, Addie. I've never known anyone stronger. Even when you were a child, you were sometimes the one holding me up. I'm glad you don't remember much about those days, but for me, it seems only yesterday. There was a hushed quality to the city after the first body was found, like we were all holding our breath. Like we somehow knew the worst was yet to come. After the second body, fear settled in, and you couldn't walk down the street without glancing over your shoulder."

Addie said, "Was my mother scared?"

"She never let on. But that was our Sandra. She was so full of bluster and bravado. I was scared for her because she fit the profile. Young, single mother living alone with an only child. On some level, she must have been frightened. David and I did our best to keep an eye on you both, but she was stubborn and independent. She refused to change her lifestyle regardless of the warnings.

'If you give in to the fear, you let him in,' she would say. And then she'd laugh and tease me. 'You worry too much, Helen. Only thirty and already you're an old fogey. Come out and have a drink with me.' And I would gently remind her that someone had to stay and watch over you. *Dear Helen. What would I ever do without you?*"

The change in her aunt's voice startled Addie, and a memory flitted. *Sometimes I think you love Helen more than me. I'm glad she's good to you, boo. I'm glad you like going to her house. But don't forget who your real mother is, okay? Don't forget me.*

"Addie?"

The sound of Helen's normal, soothing timbre chased away the memory. "Yes?"

"Where did you go just now?"

"I remembered something Mama said to me once about how much I liked being at your house. Did I stay with you often?"

"Sandra adored going out," Helen said without really answering Addie's question. "She had you when she was so young, barely eighteen, so it was only natural she'd crave a social life."

"You didn't resent having someone else's kid dumped on you? You were young, too. You and David must have had things you'd rather do than babysit me."

"Resent it? The time I spent with you was always the highlight of my week. David felt the same way. He liked having you close so that he could protect you. We were such careful people. We took every precaution. We made sure the doors and windows were locked every night, and we kept an eye out for strangers in the neighborhood. Even so, I never really believed anything could happen to someone so close to us."

"I know."

Helen gazed out toward the street, where the sun hovered just above the treetops. As the shadows grew longer, the perfume from Addie's garden deepened.

Her aunt shivered. "It's been twenty-five years, and I still get anxious this time of day."

Addie followed her gaze to the street. Two doors down, someone had come out of the house and climbed into the white van. She could hear the idle of the engine, but she couldn't make out the driver. Like the Charger she'd seen earlier, the van's windshield was tinted. Why hadn't she noticed that before?

"Do you see that van parked down the street? Was it there when you drove by?"

Helen had been lost in thought, but now she roused herself. "What? I don't know. I never even noticed it until now. But I've seen a lot of trucks and vans in front of that house since I've been feeding the strays. I'm sure it belongs to one of the workers."

"Probably, but I didn't see any logo on the side."

Helen turned to stare at her. "You're not worried about it, are you? Surely no one would be brazen enough to try to rob the place with so many people out and about."

"It wouldn't be the first time, but I'm not suggesting they're up to no good. I just like to keep an eye on any strange vehicles in the neighborhood."

"David trained you well," Helen said in approval. "He used to make me jot down make, model and license plate number if I saw anything suspicious. Now I just snap a picture with my phone. When I have one on me, that is."

"Good idea," Addie said as she took out her own phone. For the longest time, the driver remained stationary with the motor running. She thought again of that black Charger and Ethan's revelation of new evidence. Of his insistence that if something happened to him, he could trust her to do right thing.

As if drawn by the power of her stare, the van pulled onto the street and slowly came toward them.

The side window was down, but the driver wore a red cap pulled low over his brow so that Addie couldn't get a good look at him.

"That's not at all suspicious," she muttered as she lifted her phone. She zoomed in, trying to capture the rear license plate. "Did you get a glimpse of him?"

Helen didn't answer. She stared after the van for a moment, and then her hand flew to her skirt pocket as if something had suddenly occurred to her. But it was her expression that caught Addie's attention. *Stricken* was the word that came to mind.

"Aunt Helen? Are you okay? You look as if you just saw a ghost."

She turned wide eyes on Addie. "A ghost?"

"You're as white as a sheet. What's wrong? Did you recognize the driver of the van?"

"What? No. Oh, no." She shook her head as if to clear her senses. "Nothing like that. I think I remember where I left my phone."

"Where? Maybe it's still there. We can go look for it if you want."

"It's probably long gone by now, but just in case, I'll have a look on my way home. Speaking of which…" She rose and stood with her back to Addie. "I really should be going."

"I'll walk you to your car."

She seemed so tense and anxious that Addie thought she might decline. Then she relaxed when Addie slipped her arm through hers. Helen patted her hand. "Good to have you home."

"Thank you for looking after the kitties. And for the use of the cabin. It really was good to get away. I hope you and David can make it up there soon. Seems a shame to let it sit empty."

Helen glanced at her. "I'm glad you enjoyed it."

Addie searched her face. "Are you sure you're okay?"

"Yes, I'm just a little tired. I'll call you tomorrow. We'll make dinner plans."

"Just name the date."

"I'll let you get settled with your new assignment first. Addie…" Helen turned back to the street. "Be careful. I know this neighborhood isn't as dangerous as it once was, but there are bad elements everywhere these days. Keep your doors and windows locked, and turn on the alarm even when you're home. Keep your gun nearby when you sleep."

"You don't need to worry about me. As you said, David taught me well."

"Sometimes danger comes from a place you least expect," Helen said as she climbed into her car. She closed the door and lowered the window. "I'll call you about dinner."

Addie watched her back out of the drive and head down the street in the same direction as the white van. The opposite direction from Helen's neighborhood.

TWILIGHT CAME LATE and softly in the summertime. The evening breeze brought a tantalizing mixture of jasmine, moonflowers and the more elusive perfume of the tea olives. Ethan's interest in flowers was limited to his study of Orson Lee Finch. His recognition of the various scents came from Addie. She used to school him as they walked arm in arm through White Point Garden. At twenty-two, Ethan had been more interested in the scent that wafted from her long blond hair. *You're not listening to me,* she would scold him.

I'm hanging on your every word. How could I not when you have me wrapped around your little finger?

And then she would stand on tiptoes to kiss him as he threaded his fingers through that soft, soft hair, turning her face to his, kissing her back with an urgency that surprised even him.

Ethan let the memory fade as he climbed the steps to the Battery. After leaving the Gainey house, he'd gone back to his hotel to shower and change into more casual clothing, but he felt vulnerable out of his G-man uniform. The dark suits gave him a veneer of invincibility, and now in jeans and a cotton shirt, he felt increasingly unsure of himself. He had a feeling Addie would be able to see right through him, but maybe that wasn't a bad thing. He needed her on his side, and complete honesty was the only hope he had.

He trained his gaze on Charleston Harbor, marking the rise and fall of the tide as sailboats floated in the distance. He had always loved this city. His maternal grandparents were native

Charlestonians, and despite the publicity surrounding his father's breakdown and arrest, he and his mother had lived here for a time before she'd dated Richard Barrow. After their marriage, his stepfather had moved them to his home in Alexandria. He and Ethan's mother still lived in the same gleaming white colonial. To anyone unaware of the backstory, they seemed an idyllic family, and yet even as a kid, Ethan had felt like an impostor.

Sensing eyes on him, he turned his head, almost expecting to find his counterparts in dark suits and sunglasses watching him. Instead, he saw Addie making her way through the evening crowd. She'd gone home to change and now, in cutoffs and sneakers, she looked more like a college kid than a seasoned police detective. She'd pulled her hair back and tucked it up loosely at her nape. She wore sunglasses, too, so he couldn't see her eyes, but she wasn't smiling. Her sober demeanor took nothing away from her attractiveness. She looked fit, tanned and ready to take on the world. Or him.

Ethan turned back to the water, collecting his thoughts and emotions as he waited for her to approach.

"I wasn't sure you'd come," he said, his gaze still on the distant sails. He turned slowly to face her, eyeing her leisurely from behind his own dark glasses.

"I told you I would. I always try to keep my word." She moved up beside him at the rail. "You're early, I see."

"I didn't want to take a chance on missing you. I know this can't be easy. The way things went down between us—"

She glanced away. "I don't want to talk about that. That's not why I'm here. You said you had information about my mother's murder. I don't know what you could have possibly dug up after all this time, but here I am, so let's get to it."

He flicked a glance behind her down the crowded walkway. "Not much privacy out here. Are you sure you don't want a drink or a bite to eat? We could go to Pearlz."

"I'm not going to eat or drink with you, Ethan. This isn't a date."

"I didn't mean to imply that it was. Can we at least go across the street to the park and find a quiet bench?"

Her mouth tightened as she reached up to tuck back a strand of hair. "Fine."

They went down the steps and crossed East Bay, keeping a careful distance between them. Ethan could still smell jasmine on the warm breeze that blew across the harbor. The scent and the woman beside him stirred memories he'd tried to keep buried for ten long years, ever since that final showdown when Addie had made it clear she never wanted to see him again. He could still remember the glitter of angry tears in her eyes and the faint quiver of her lip before she'd turned and walked away. They'd both been so young, and Ethan had made so many mistakes. Maybe it was fitting that Orson Lee Finch's words should once again come back to haunt him. *A man like you will always be at war with his emotions. Tormented by what he can't know. Unable to make peace with his past.*

Addie stopped in front of a bench facing the street. "This okay with you?"

Her voice snapped him back to the present. "Yes, fine. The shade feels good."

She waited until he responded before settling herself at one end of the bench. He joined her, draping one arm across the back. Addie took off her sunglasses and laid them on the seat between them as if to create a physical barrier.

For a moment, neither of them spoke. Ethan wondered if she were as lost in the past as he was. If she remembered all those moonlit drives, the walks on the beach, the nights spent in her garage apartment off Morrison Drive. Now she lived in a small East Side house with a mortgage, but she wouldn't like him knowing that.

He felt her gaze on him and turned to find her eyes slightly narrowed as she studied him. Then she glanced at her watch. "I don't have long. We should get started."

He wanted to ask if she had a date later that

evening, but instead he nodded. "To explain the new evidence, we'll have to talk about the crime scene. I'm sorry. I know that'll be painful for you."

"And for you," she said, her gaze lifting to meet his. Her expression was not without compassion. "Go on."

"Three DNA samples were collected at that scene. Your mother's, my father's and a third blood sample that was never identified."

"Both the police and FBI concluded the un-identified DNA had been in the alley before the murder."

"A reasonable explanation, but that sample has always tormented me, even though nothing ever turned up in the databases."

"It was your obsession," Addie murmured.

She would remember, because she'd suffered the consequences of that obsession. "My father's erratic behavior at the time of his arrest and his subsequent mental breakdown made it all too easy to accept him as the murderer, especially since his abilities as a profiler enabled him to mimic the Twilight Killer's MO. That MO included things that hadn't been released to the public at the time. The staging of the bodies, for example. But my father wasn't the only one who had access to that information."

"You're leaving out the most damning pieces of evidence," Addie said. "Not only was James Merrick's DNA found at the crime scene, the murder weapon was located two blocks from his hotel and his bloody clothing was found in the hotel dumpster."

"My father was a brilliant man. He knew the criminal mind better than anyone of his time. It's hard to imagine he would make such careless mistakes."

"But that was his whole defense," Addie reminded him. "He wasn't in his right mind. You said yourself his behavior was erratic at the time of his arrest and he subsequently suffered a complete mental breakdown."

An exasperated edge crept into Ethan's tone despite his best efforts at neutrality. "Those discoveries were too convenient. If he still had enough rational thought to remove the murder weapon from the crime scene, why dispose of it in such an obvious location rather than tossing it in the harbor? Why not burn the bloody clothing? None of this has ever made sense to me."

"What puzzles you the most?" Addie demanded. "That he was careless in disposing of evidence or that he killed my mother in cold blood?"

That was blunt.

Ethan inwardly winced. The meeting wasn't going well. Far from breaking down barriers, he had forced her to put up more walls. She was withdrawn and defensive, and he wondered if he'd made a mistake coming to her with what he'd found. Who else would believe him, though? Whom could he trust to help him dig for the truth if not the victim's child?

"I'm sorry," he said. "I didn't mean to get into any of that. I just wanted to remind you about the third DNA sample."

She made an impatient gesture with her hand. "Got it. Keep going."

"Two weeks ago, I received an email from a genealogist here in Charleston who claimed she'd cross-referenced the third DNA sample against a number of public databases. She got a match."

Addie whirled, her eyes going wide with disbelief. *"What?"*

Ethan nodded. "Thousands of those databases exit, created mostly by people who post their DNA profiles online in the hopes of finding long-lost relatives. Biological mothers and adopted children, for example."

"Now that doesn't make any sense to me," Addie said. "I don't mean the part about the databases or long-lost relatives. I'm talking about the sample itself. How would a genealogist get her hands on DNA evidence that's been in police custody for over twenty-five years?"

"I think she or someone close to her had a connection in the police department."

Addie frowned. "You think a cop gave her the sample?"

"She may have had it for years with no way

to check for a match. These public databases are fairly new technology."

"Did you ask her where she got the sample?"

"Yes, but she was guarded. She refused to provide details through email or over the phone. She insisted I come to Charleston to meet with her in person."

"And that didn't set off any alarm bells for you?"

"Her credentials checked out. She said she needed to be discreet because if anyone found out about her research, her life could be in danger."

"And you believed her?"

"I didn't at first. I thought she was exaggerating to coerce my cooperation. We emailed back and forth a few times, and then the correspondence just stopped. I told myself to let it go. No good could come from digging all that up again, but—"

"You couldn't."

He shrugged. "When she didn't answer my emails, I made some inquiries. I found out she'd been killed in a hit-and-run two days after she first made contact with me."

Addie stared at him for the longest moment. Then she asked in a strained tone, "What was her name?"

"Naomi Quinlan. She taught night courses on genealogy research at the community college. She was struck while walking home from class one evening."

"Quinlan, Quinlan," Addie muttered. "I know

that name. I remember that hit-and-run. It happened right off King Street. I caught the call, but another detective was already on the scene by the time I got there. It was bad. The impact was so severe the coroner said she probably died instantly. There were no witnesses, nothing at the scene or in the victim's history to support premeditation. We assumed the driver was under the influence and lost control of the vehicle."

"The driver has never been found?"

"Not as far as I know."

"You said you caught the call. Why didn't you lead the investigation?"

"Like I said, another detective was already on the scene, so I backed off because I was being transferred out of the Investigations Bureau, anyway."

"Why?"

"New assignment."

"So you never followed up on the hit-and-run?"

"I had my hands full trying to clear the active cases on my desk." But remorse flashed in her eyes before she turned to stare at the street.

"I understand," Ethan said. "Never enough hours in the day. When I tried to press Naomi for the name of the DNA donor, she reminded me that careers had been built on the Twilight Killer case and on my father's subsequent arrest. If either investigation was discredited by a new piece of evidence, a lot of important reputations would be tarnished."

"That sounds a bit dramatic," Addie said.

"I thought so, too. Right up until the time she turned up dead."

Addie frowned. "You don't know that her death was related to the DNA match. That hit-and-run could have been nothing more than a tragic accident. The driver panicked and fled. Coincidences do happen, you know."

"Are you trying to convince me or yourself?"

She looked annoyed. "Okay, let's break it down. Naomi Quinlan claimed she got a hit from a public database, but she wouldn't provide you with any of the details. She wouldn't tell you how she obtained the DNA sample or the name of the donor match. Isn't it possible she was just messing with you, Ethan? There are a lot of sick people in this world. I still get anonymous letters around this time of year. And now, with all the hoopla surrounding the twenty-fifth anniversary, I expect crackpots will be crawling out of the woodwork."

Ethan's voice sharpened. "You get anonymous letters? What do they say?"

Addie tucked back her hair. "Nothing important. What matters is this woman's motive and her timing. Why now, with the anniversary looming? Is it possible she wanted to inject herself into a famous case for the notoriety? You are James Merrick's son. She wouldn't have had to do much digging to find you, even with the name change. It's just all very curious—convenient, to use your descriptor—that she was able to get a match when CODIS has never turned up a single hit."

"If the unsub doesn't have an arrest record, he or she wouldn't be in any LE database," Ethan said.

"True. But why would someone who left DNA at a murder scene knowingly allow their genetic profile to be publicly cataloged?"

"I've given that a lot of thought," Ethan said. "The unsub may not have realized he'd been wounded. Adrenaline blocks pain, and a thrill kill produces euphoria. Sometimes an almost fugue state of rapture. And remember, the third blood sample was never made public, so the unsub had no reason to believe his DNA could be traced back to the crime scene."

"You have given this thought."

"Yes, and having said all that, I think there's a more logical explanation. Naomi Quinlan's hit was only a partial match. Familial DNA."

"That's a slippery slope," Addie said.

"For law enforcement, yes. Some states are more stringent about such searches than others. They require that the criminal and the person in the database share an identical Y chromosome, which means the match is limited to men. But a genealogist is under no such constraint. She could have cast a wide net."

"That kind of scattershot approach produces a lot of false positives. You know that as well as I do."

"Depends on how closely the samples matched up."

Addie scowled at him in the fading light. "You're playing with fire, Ethan. This is the kind of thing that got us both into a lot of trouble ten years ago. Some days I feel as if I'm still wading out of that mess. What are the chances you'll forget all about Naomi Quinlan and go back to Quantico?"

"Zero."

She sighed. "I figured. And just what is it you expect me to do?"

"Nothing. I don't expect anything from you. I just wanted you to have this information in case—"

"Nothing is going to happen to you."

She said it so fiercely, he almost believed her. "I know you want to believe that justice was served in your mother's case, but what if it wasn't? What if her killer is still out there somewhere? Can you live with that possibility?"

She turned on him in anger. "That's not a fair question. You've given me nothing but supposition. You have no real proof."

"That's why I'm here in Charleston. If proof exists, I'll find it." He sat back against the bench, casting a wary glance around the park.

He couldn't detect surveillance, but that didn't mean they were alone. "I've gone over the emails time and again. Naomi Quinlan had a strange way with words and syntax. It's possible she left clues that I haven't yet been able to decipher."

Addie was still angry. "Do you even realize how that sounds?"

"The Unabomber was caught by the way he turned a phrase."

She merely shook her head and stood. "I've heard you out. Now I need to get back."

Ethan rose, too. He shoved his hands in his pockets as he stood facing her. "Thanks for coming. Thanks for listening."

"Nothing's changed for me. You need to know that."

A breeze blew in from the sea, ruffling her hair as her gaze reluctantly met his. A moment passed, and then another, and still she remained. Ethan's blood quickened, but he didn't move toward her. He knew better. It was too soon. And yet…

"Addie—"

Her voice slipped out on a whisper. "Don't, Ethan." She turned away. "Don't do anything stupid."

Chapter Five

Darkness had fallen by the time Addie got home.
She parked in the garage and then let herself out
the side door to the backyard. The moment she
stepped onto the walkway, a motion-detector light
came on to illuminate the space between the garage and the house. She wasn't afraid of the dark.
She was a trained LEO, and she was on her home
turf. Still, precaution was never a bad thing. Distractions could be deadly. It would be too easy
to get preoccupied by Ethan's disclosures—or, if
she were honest, by his mere presence —so she
needed to be on guard for any lapses.

A decade was a long time, and Addie had been
over Ethan for most of those years. How could one
cling to something that had never been real? She'd
fallen in love with Ethan Barrow, not realizing
that Ethan Merrick was part of the package. The
son of her mother's killer. Even now their union
seemed surreal. How could she not have known
what he really wanted from her? How could she
not have recognized that his obsession to clear

his father's name was so great, he'd wittingly se-
duced her into his delusions? Not that she was
blameless. At twenty-two and freshly graduated
from the police academy, she should have been
sharper, her radar more finely tuned. She should
have seen right through Ethan Barrow's deception, but no. One smile, one brooding look, and
she'd been lost.

Everyone's heart got broken sooner or later.
Addie forgave herself for falling for the wrong
man. She allowed herself a pass for buying into
his lies and deceit. What she could never forgive
was her own lies. Her betrayal of the one man
who had always had her back.

*You've let me down, Addie. And worse, you've
let yourself down. I can't even begin to tell you
how disappointed I am in you. You used my computer, my password to access sealed files, and
then you allowed classified information to be
leaked to the press, calling this department's integrity into question. If it were anyone else, you
would have already been dismissed. But I know
your potential and I know, in time, you can be a
great asset. I'm willing to look the other way this
once, but from now on, your conduct will be ex-
emplary, no exceptions or excuses, and you will
work twice as hard as anyone else in your unit.
I'm giving you a second chance. The rest is up
to you.*

From now on, in my office and at this station,

*I'm Deputy Chief Cutler, even when we're alone.
Are we clear?*

A hard lesson learned, but Addie had become
a better cop, a better person for it. In time, she'd
earned the respect of her partner, her captain and
the deputy chief, and now she wasn't about to
squander their trust, no matter how much Ethan's
revelations niggled.

One of the strays she fed stole out of the bushes
to greet her, and as Addie bent to pet the still
skittish feline, she saw deep red splotches on the
walkway. She thought at first one of the cats had
been wounded, and her heart catapulted to her
throat. In the next instant, she realized the spots
were flower petals, crimson and fragrant and
every bit as unnerving as drops of blood. She
lifted one of the petals to her nose. The scent of
magnolia overwhelmed her, and she found herself
drowning in dread and old memories.

She rose, still half crouching, and slipped
into the shadows. The cat followed her, rubbing
against her legs and meowing for more attention.

"Quiet," Addie whispered. She glanced around
the yard, senses on full alert. She could hear traffic on a distant street and the trill of some night
bird. Sensing her tension, the cat had gone quiet
at her feet. Addie remained sequestered for another moment before slipping from the shadows to
hurry up the back steps. The door was still locked,
and another security light came on, drenching her

in illumination. She went back down the steps and circled the house, checking windows along the way until she reached the front entrance. That door was locked as well.

Even so, she remained tense and alert as she entered the house. A lamp in the small foyer was on a timer, and she was grateful for the soft glow that chased away shadows. She hurried over to a small desk, typed in the code on her security console and then unlocked the top drawer, where she kept a gun. Her service weapon was in her bedroom, locked in a nightstand.

Right hand supported with her left, she moved through the house, checking corners and closets, doors and windows until she was satisfied that no one had entered her home.

Grabbing a flashlight from the kitchen, she went out the back door to have another look around. Angling the light along the flagstones, she traced the crimson trail from the steps all the way back to the garage. No way she could have missed those petals, and no doubt they had been left for her to find.

She kept the gun in her right hand while she lifted the flashlight with her left, sweeping the beam back toward the fence where the floodlights didn't reach. A breeze rattled the palmettos, and she could hear the soft mewling of the cat somewhere in the bushes. But all else was quiet. Too quiet.

The hair at the back of Addie's neck lifted as she scanned the shadows. She wanted to believe the petals were nothing but a cruel prank. Like the anonymous letters she received from time to time, the magnolia trail meant nothing. But she couldn't forget Ethan's suggestion that her mother's killer might still be out there. What if he had been keeping tabs on Addie all these years? What if, like Delmar Gainey, he still thrilled to his dark secrets?

The notion of someone deriving pleasure from spying on the daughter of his victim was more than Addie wanted to contemplate at the moment. She'd had enough monsters for one day. Turning, she moved back along the path to the steps, but as the light swung back into the yard, the beam clipped a silhouette against the fence. Just a tree, Addie told herself. *Just a shadow.*

Slowly, she moved the light back over the yard, catching the gleam of human eyes before the figure turned and scrambled over her fence.

"Stop!" Before she had time to consider her actions, Addie sprinted after him, tucking her weapon and flashlight in the waistband of her shorts so that she could hoist herself up and over the fence. She landed with a thud in her neighbor's backyard. Drawing her weapon, she hunkered in the shadows at the fence, peering into the darkness for any sign of her trespasser.

Her neighbor's yard was dark, and only a faint

glow emanated from the edges of the closed blinds. Now Addie was the trespasser. She told herself to give up the chase and go home. She could call for a patrol of the street, but the intruder would be long gone by the time a unit was dispatched to the scene. Better she check this out for herself. At the very least, she could give the trespasser second thoughts about invading her turf again.

A dog barked down the street. The same night bird trilled from a treetop. Addie waited. Across the yard came the sound of rustling leaves, followed by a scrape. Heart still thudding, she pinpointed the noise with her flashlight, glimpsing the back of the intruder as he went over the fence into the yard of the house being renovated. No one would be around at this hour. A vacant house would be the perfect place to hide.

Again, Addie told herself to give it up. She'd scared him sufficiently by now. *Go home. Go to bed. Let it go.*

But she couldn't let it go. Her stubbornness propelled her over the second fence, and she dropped to the ground more lightly this time. Hugging the bushes, she took out her phone and texted the address to Matt Lepear.

She slipped the phone back into her pocket and eased across the yard, flashlight over gun. The back door hung open. Not a good sign. Nor were the magnolia petals that had been dropped along the back steps. The intruder was outright taunting her now. Aggressively so.

Protocol and common sense demanded Addie wait for backup. She went up the steps without hesitation, flattening herself against the wall for a moment before proceeding inside. She moved through the open floor plan quickly, clearing each space before entering the next. An empty paint can clanged against her toe, and she crouched as she swept the area with the flashlight.

"I know you're in here," she said. "Show yourself. I just want to talk."

"Adaline." The electronically distorted voice was so low she couldn't tell where the sound came from. Dread descended as she moved through the shadows.

"Who are you?" she demanded.

No answer.

"How do you know me?"

Silence.

"Why did you leave those magnolia petals on my walkway?"

"You know why."

The warped voice echoed through the empty room, sending chills up and down Addie's spine. "Come out now and deal with me, or deal with my backup."

She eased through the plastic partitions, listening for a misplaced step or a telltale breath. All was silent. She had a feeling he could see her, though. That he was watching her every move. She glanced over her shoulder, glanced all around her. He was *there*. She couldn't see him, couldn't hear him, but she sensed his presence. He was close.

Something metallic pinged against the floor, and Addie whirled, moving quickly through the plastic sheets until she realized too late that she'd walked into his trap. She'd let him distract her, and now he'd come up behind her.

She turned, catching only a glimpse of a masked face before the intruder struck her across the forehead with the flat side of a board. The blow dazed her, and she staggered back, dropping the flashlight as she crashed to the floor. The partitions came down on top of her, and for a moment, Addie panicked, clawing like a caged tiger at her plastic prison. She fought her way up and scrambled free, reaching for her weapon as she heard footsteps running from the room, down the hall, out the front door.

Scrambling to her feet, she attempted to pursue, but the blow had stunned her and he had too much of a head start. She trailed him onto the front porch, angling the light over the yard and down the street.

Then she collapsed on the front steps to wait for her partner.

ADDIE SAT ON the edge of the bathtub and winced as Matt Lepear cleaned the cut on her forehead and then applied a butterfly bandage. He was none too gentle about it, either. "You don't need stitches, but that's going to leave an ugly mark. You're lucky he didn't take out an eye."

"I guess this is my day for close calls." She touched the bandage gingerly. "Thanks for doctoring me up. And for getting here so quickly."

"I was at Shorty's," he said, naming a nearby watering hole. "You should have waited until I got here. What you did was really stupid. You know that, right?"

Addie shrugged. "You would have done the same thing."

"I would have had the good sense not to get myself coldcocked before help arrived." He put away the supplies and then rinsed his hands at the sink. "Okay, now that you have my undivided attention, walk me through what happened. Start at the beginning, when you first saw the flower petals."

"Not just any flower petals. Crimson magnolia petals." A shudder went through Addie as she folded her arms around her middle.

"I get the significance," he said with a nod. "The Twilight Killer was a gardener. He studied horticulture in college. They covered all that in the documentary. His schooling. His resentment of the elite and his fixation on single mothers. The particular kind of red magnolia he grew was rare. The crimson petals became his signature.

And now someone has left those same magnolia petals on your walkway."

"The same color, at least. We don't know if they're precisely the same. There are dozens of varieties of red magnolias. I admit I was jolted when I saw them—I thought they were drops of blood at first—but now I just think it was someone's idea of a prank. That's why he hung around to witness my reaction. I'm sure he didn't count on my chasing after him."

"He knew your name, though. You said he called you Adaline."

"He would have to know my name to find my address. Maybe he watched the same documentary you did. Saw my picture and decided to have a little sick fun."

"Sick sounds about right."

Addie stood and brushed off her shorts. "You want a beer?"

"I never turn down a cold one. But I have to say, you seem pretty calm about all this."

"It's not even close to the worst thing I've seen today." She checked his handiwork in the mirror before exiting the bathroom behind him. Matt knew her house well enough to take the lead down the hallway and into the kitchen. He sat on a bar stool while she grabbed icy bottles from the refrigerator and uncapped them. Then she went around the bar to join him.

"Do you think this incident could have something to do with why Ethan Barrow's back in town?"

Addie slid over a coaster. "I don't see how."

"It seems a big coincidence, all this happening to you tonight after he showed up today."

"Oh, come on," Addie said. "You don't seriously think he did this."

"Not him personally, no. But he has a way of bringing trouble. Why's he here, anyway?"

"He said he had business with the deputy chief." The half-truth slipped a little too easily through Addie's lips, especially for someone who had always tried to be totally honest with her partner. Matt would see through her, of course, but Addie wasn't sure she was ready to get into the whole Ethan Barrow discussion. The meeting with him had affected her more than she wanted to admit. Memories were stirring, and it was hard enough to keep them at bay without his name popping up all over the place.

Matt eyed her dubiously. "What business?"

"He didn't elaborate. He said it would be up to my uncle to tell me."

"Okay, then. Let me put it another way. Why did he come to see *you*? And how did he know you'd be at the Gainey house?"

"Apparently, he overheard someone at the station mention my whereabouts."

"So he just showed up out of the blue? Without any prior conversations or correspondence? Just boom, he's here." Matt gave her a long scrutiny. "Sorry, Add. Not buying it. You're being cagey as hell. That man's here for a reason, and my guess is, that reason is you."

Addie was quick to dispel him. "He's not here because of me. Not in the way you're implying."

"Then what way is it? I don't mean to get all up in your business, but he caused a lot of trouble for a lot of people. If you've got something going with him—"

"I don't. God, no. Why would you even think that?"

Matt shrugged. "I watched the two of you together earlier. I could be way off, but I'm not so sure all those feelings are dead, at least on his end. I saw the way he looked at you."

"He doesn't still have feelings for me," Addie insisted. "How could he? Until today, he hadn't even seen me in ten years."

"It's called carrying a torch."

"And you would be familiar with that term, since you're dating your ex-wife."

He touched his bottle to hers.

Addie couldn't help but grin. "How is Maggie, by the way?"

"*Amber's* fine. Sends her regards. But let's not change the subject. You say there's nothing romantic between you and Barrow, and I believe you. There's nothing going on *yet*. But you need to watch your back, Addie. He knows how to push your buttons. I don't trust him, and neither should you."

"I will and I don't. No need to worry about me."

"Says the woman who pursued a suspect into an empty building without backup."

"Trespasser. I pursued a trespasser. Not like he shot anyone."

"That you know of. Are you going to file a report?"

"You know how much I hate paperwork," Addie said with a grimace. "Besides, he's long gone, and I doubt he'll be back."

"You never know. Might be a good idea to get proactive." Matt lifted his beer. "Ever think about installing security cameras around the perimeter of your house? If he does come back, you could catch him in the act."

Addie shrugged. "I like the idea, but that's an expense I don't need right now."

"They may not be as pricey as you think. My cousin sells all kinds of security equipment. I can get you a discount. And I have a buddy who owes me a favor. He'll install them for free if you keep the beer flowing."

"That's a nice offer," Addie said. "I'll think about it. It may not be necessary, though. As soon as the anniversary drama dies down, the crazies will crawl back into their basements. At least until next year."

"What do you mean, until next year? This kind of thing has happened before?"

"Not the flower petals, but I've received a few anonymous letters over the years. I blame the media. They're the ones that coined the whole Twilight's Children thing. They created this mystical narrative around the murdered mothers and their surviving offspring, and we became these cultlike figures. You wouldn't believe the weirdos who follow me on social media. Someone even named a rock band after us. It's bizarre and beyond creepy."

Matt scowled in disapproval. "What did the letters say? And why did you never mention them before?"

"I didn't think they were important. Just nonsensical ramblings, usually from someone claiming to be the real Twilight Killer. Or someone claiming to be in love with the Twilight Killer. Strangely, I've never received a letter from anyone claiming to be James Merrick."

"Maybe that's a good thing," Matt said. "Merrick's son did enough damage."

"Dead horse. Let's not go there again." Addie got up and went into the kitchen. "Another round?"

"I'd better finish this one and head home." But he seemed in no hurry to leave. "I'd still like to know what Ethan Barrow is doing in Charleston."

Addie rolled her eyes. "You're really not going

to leave this alone, are you? All right, just think about it for a minute. It doesn't take a clairvoyant to figure out Ethan's motives. He's still looking for answers. He's never believed his father was guilty."

Matt studiously picked at the beer label with his thumbnail. "Yeah, I figured. But maybe his concern runs deeper than a desire to clear dear old dad."

"What do you mean?"

His gaze lifted. "*You* think about it, Addie. How would you feel if you were in his position? He's not much younger than his father was when he went off the deep end. With each year that passes, Ethan has to be worried about his genes. He's not just trying to clear his old man. He's trying to convince himself the same thing won't happen to him."

Addie had entertained similar theories over the years, but Matt's ability to cut through the clutter and niceties hit her like a physical blow. She felt stunned, though she did her best to shrug off his reasoning. "I'm the last person to defend James Merrick, but he had a lot of outside stressors. His job, a troubled marriage, childhood abuse. Drug use, too, if the rumors are to be believed. It all came to a head during his investigation of Orson Lee Finch. Somehow he began to identify with the monster he hunted. The experts said he suffered from a kind of trauma bond that compelled him to finish the killer's mission. Ethan has no reason to believe the same thing could happen to him."

"I don't know," Matt said. "Dude's wound pretty tight, if you ask me. Maybe there's more to his behavior than stubbornness or even obsession. Maybe something darker rides along with him."

His words chilled Addie more than she wanted to admit. "And with that, we've officially exhausted the subject of Ethan Barrow." She made a production of stretching. "I think we should call it a night."

"Kicking me out, eh? Did I touch a nerve?"

"No, but you already said you needed to hit the road—"

She broke off as a loud crash sounded outside. They drew their weapons simultaneously. Addie turned off the kitchen light and then trailed Matt to the back door.

"Can you see anything?" she whispered.

"Not much." He opened the door, and they slipped through. "You need better lighting out here."

"The floodlight should have come on," Addie muttered as they went down the steps together.

The breeze had risen while they were inside. Addie thought at first a tree branch had fallen on the garage roof and taken out the security light. But the wind wasn't that strong.

"Matt." She tapped his arm. "Check out the garage. The security light is broken."

He angled his gun and the flashlight in that direction, picking up the trail of crimson petals before shifting the light to the garage door and then up to the eaves, where nothing but a shard of glass protruded from the light socket. He tried the garage door and then shone the light through the glass panel.

While he checked out the garage, Addie hunkered on the walkway to examine the shattered glass. "That bulb didn't break itself."

"Someone deliberately took it out," Matt said. "You still think this is all just a bad joke?"

She glanced up. "How soon can your friend come and install those security cams?"

ETHAN WAS SURPRISED to find Gwen Holloway waiting for him in the lobby of his hotel when he got back from his meeting with Addie. He'd stopped for takeout, and now all he wanted to do was head upstairs, eat his sandwich and go back over Naomi Quinlan's emails, searching for those elusive clues. Maybe Addie was right. Maybe he really was grasping at straws, but it only made sense that the genealogist would have left bread crumbs if she believed her life could be in danger.

He thought about trying to slip past the former agent, but she was planted near the elevators, making avoidance impossible unless he exited the hotel. But that would only postpone the inevitable. She'd wait him out tonight or have her people track him down in the morning. She was that tenacious.

Ethan resolved himself to the confrontation. Gwen Holloway hadn't been on the federal payroll in nearly fifteen years, but she still had powerful connections inside the Bureau and the DOJ. One call and she could make his life uncomfortable if not downright miserable.

These days, she traveled the country teaching and consulting with various law enforcement entities, but she still dressed in the traditional FBI uniform of a plain black suit, white blouse and polished loafers. In her fifties, she'd refused to cut her waist-length brown hair, compromising instead by pulling it back from her face and securing it in a bun at her nape. She wore no makeup, but her nails were always immaculately groomed and her teeth were almost blindingly white, though she rarely smiled.

She came toward Ethan now, her gaze so intently focused she might have been vectoring in on one of the FBI's most wanted. "Hello, Ethan. Do you have time for a chat?"

"Sorry." He held up his takeout bag. "I'm having dinner in my room and calling it a night. Maybe another time."

He might have been addressing a wall. She turned on her heel and said over her shoulder, "There's a coffee shop just down the street. It should be nice and quiet this time of day."

Ethan hesitated for only a moment before he followed her back out into the warm evening air. She was a tall woman, and he matched his stride to hers, the brisk pace drawing a few glances from the strolling tourists. There was still quite a bit of traffic for a Friday night. Delectable aromas wafted from restaurants as laughter and music spilled out from bars. People were in good spirits, anticipating the weekend. The afternoon had been hot and humid, but twilight brought sea breezes and cooling temperatures. This was the time of day that Charleston did best. Good food, strong drinks and interesting company.

Nostalgia stirred, and Ethan found himself once again thinking about Addie. She looked good. The years since their breakup had only enhanced her appeal. She was leaner than he remembered, her toned muscles a testament to the time she dedicated to the track and to the gym. She still wore her blond hair long, though like Gwen Holloway, she pulled it back and up so that her periphery was unimpeded.

Seeing her again had brought back a lot of mixed emotions. Ethan supposed he'd never really gotten over her, though he hadn't pined for her. Pining was an indulgence and a dangerous distraction for someone in his line of work. Yet for the first few months after the breakup, rarely a day had gone by that he hadn't berated himself for what he'd done. Remorse had been an unwelcome companion. But ten years was a long time, and he'd moved on even if those regrets still surfaced now and then. Even if Adaline Kinsella still popped into his head at the most unexpected times.

No, he hadn't pined. He'd thrown himself into his work and recommitted himself to his training. He'd dated. He'd even had a serious relationship, but things had eventually gone flat, and they'd ended things amicably. The romance had never progressed beyond a certain point, and truth be told, she'd never measured up to Addie. In hindsight, Ethan realized that he was the one who hadn't measured up. Comparisons to Addie had been an excuse. Someone like him was probably better off alone.

He hadn't pined for Addie then and he didn't pine for her now, even on a crowded street when loneliness seemed to weigh on him the heaviest.

"Ethan? What's wrong with you? I said your name three times just now and you ignored me."

"Sorry." He shook himself out of his fog as a black Charger came into his line of sight. It was parked at the curb with the windows up and the motor running. "I was just checking out that car across the street. Government issued, looks like. Your people?"

Gwen barely glanced at the car. "What makes you think so?"

"Wild guess." He tossed his unopened sandwich in a nearby trash bin. "Makes me wonder what ordinary citizens would think if they knew certain former federal agents were allowed to call up the FBI and request surveillance on one of their own, all on the taxpayers' dime."

"What makes you think I'm the one who made that call?"

He gave her a sidelong glance. "Who then? My stepfather?"

"There are a lot of powerful people who like to keep tabs on you, Ethan."

"Why? I'm nothing special."

She returned his side-eye. "We both know that's not true."

"I get it. The interest comes from people in the Bureau and the DOJ who don't think of me as Ethan Barrow. To them, I'll always be James Merrick's son. Do you all sit around wondering when I'll crack?"

"If we wondered that, you wouldn't be where you are today. But we do have concerns about your recent behavior. Like it or not, your presence in this city attracts attention. Last time you were here, you compromised the Bureau's relationship with local law enforcement, embarrassed your family and nearly got yourself fired. You leaked information about procedure and blood evidence that allowed the press to question the results of a long and painful investigation. Your stepfather and I went out on a limb for you." She glanced both ways before she stepped into the intersection. "You were given a second chance on our recommendation, so don't act like we're an inconvenience when we expect answers."

"What's the question?"

"Why are you in Charleston?"

He gave a careless shrug. "Just relaxing and taking in the sights."

"I hear you were also taking in the sights in Columbia yesterday." She smoothed back her wind-ruffled hair. "How is James, by the way?"

"About as well as you would expect for someone who has spent the last twenty-five years confined to a psychiatric unit for the criminally insane. But maybe you should go and judge his condition for yourself."

"I have."

He turned. "When?"

"I've gone to see him regularly since the day he was committed." She stopped in front of the coffee shop and waited for Ethan to open the door. For some reason, that surprised him, though he complied without hesitation. Gwen glanced back at him. "You're not the only one who still cares about him, you know."

She stepped inside, holding up two fingers to the barista and then pointing to a table in the back. She slid into the seat facing the door, leaving Ethan to sit with his back exposed. That did not surprise him.

"When was the last time you saw him?" he pressed.

"It's been a while. Almost a year." She shrugged off her jacket and hung it on the back of her chair. She folded her arms on the table and clasped her hands. He could see bits of gold shimmering around her throat and in her ears, but her fingers were bare. She was a handsome, accomplished woman—a successful author and wealthy entrepreneur—but she'd never married. Ethan could understand why. Dating didn't come easy to those who spent their lives hunting monsters.

She gazed at him across the table, silent until their coffee had been served, and then she said, "Are you upset that I still visit him?"

"Why would I be upset?"

"I don't know, Ethan. Why don't you tell me? Maybe it's a proprietary thing. I can sense your hostility. You used to be better at hiding it."

"I don't know what you mean."

Her hazel eyes watched him closely. "I've known you since you were a child. I've watched you grow up. Your parents graciously included me in the milestones of your life, but you always resented my presence, didn't you?"

"Then why come if you knew you weren't welcome?"

"Because Richard and Karen were my friends

and because I cared about you. I still do. I understand the nature of your resentment, even if you don't. Deep down, you blame me for what happened to your father. Rationally, you know that I was just doing my job. That I never wanted any of that for him or for you. But emotionally..." She sighed. "It's still very painful for me, too, Ethan. James was not only my mentor, but also my friend. His absence and his legacy will always be felt in the BAU. And by me."

"You left quite a legacy yourself."

"I like to think so."

Ethan stared back at her. "You were with the FBI for, what? Ten years before you left to write your first book? You were on a fast track. Unit chief, destined to be section chief, maybe even deputy director by now. Everyone must have been stunned when you tendered your resignation."

"Not really. The BAU has a high burnout rate. You should know that better than most. I didn't leave to write a book or even to start my own firm. I wanted to get my life back. And I felt I could be just as effective on the outside as a teacher and consultant, maybe more so. What's your point, anyway?"

"There's no point." Ethan glanced out the window, searching the street for signs of surveillance. The black Charger was nowhere in sight. He wondered if Gwen had covertly signaled the agents to back off. "It's just something I've thought about over the years. You were my father's protégée. The two of you were very close, and yet you didn't hesitate to profile him."

"He would have done the same to me."

"Not one moment of self-doubt or second thought? Even when you all but led the Charleston PD to his doorstep?"

Something flickered in the green-gold depths of her eyes. Anger, Ethan thought, but not remorse. The Gwen Holloways of the world didn't look back with regret. "I trusted the profile," she said.

"That profile and his arrest made you famous. You became a household name. A Bureau rock star. The young agent who brought down the great James Merrick."

"Again, what's your point?"

"What if your profile was wrong?"

"The evidence wasn't wrong."

"Evidence can be planted."

Ethan could see the wheels turning inside her head as she sifted back through their conversation, deciding on the best way to handle him. She landed on bemused empathy. "You've been holding all this in for a very long time, haven't you? That's not good on any level. You should have come to me instead of letting all this fester." She cupped her hands around her coffee cup, but she didn't drink. "If you've got more to say, now's the time to let it out. Tell me everything. Let's clear the air once and for all."

"You know I can't do that."

"Why hold back now? It's not like I can hurt you. I haven't worked for the government in years. I have no control over your life or your career. You and I are just friends."

Ethan's voice hardened despite his best efforts. He didn't want to reveal any cracks. She would pounce the moment she sensed weakness. "We're not friends," he said. "And we both know you could end my career with one phone call."

"You think I'm that thin-skinned and vindictive?" She lifted her cup with another sigh. "Believe it or not, I've always had your back, Ethan. I've always been your champion, just as James once championed me. I'm giving you a free pass. Speak your mind. You have my guarantee that nothing you say will leave this table or be used against you."

Ethan leaned back in his chair, slipping one hand in his pocket as he regarded her with wary curiosity. What was she up to? "You mean that?"

"I do. I'd really like to explore the origins of your hostility."

"Then instead of talking about the profile and my father's confinement, maybe we should talk about your affair."

Emotion flickered across her face, but to her credit, she never broke eye contact. "That's nonsense."

"I saw the two of you together."

"Of course you did. We worked together."

"No, this was different. I saw you in my grandparents' garden here in Charleston. My mother and I came down one weekend during the Twilight Killer investigation. My father had been gone for weeks, and my mother begged him to have dinner with us on our last night because we wouldn't see him again for a long time. He finally relented and even brought a change of clothing so that he could stay over. I heard him leave in the middle of the night. I got up and followed him out. I wanted to talk him into staying so that my mother wouldn't be so unhappy when she woke up. You were waiting for him in the garden. You tried to kiss him, but he pushed you away. He said it was over. He thought it best that you transfer out of the unit. You got angry, and then you got violent. You slapped him, as I recall. I think you even clawed his face. I didn't understand a lot of what went down between you, but your outburst scared me."

"Why didn't you say anything?"

"I don't know. I just knew that it was a bad thing and that if I told my mother, she would be hurt. It was only when I grew older and looked back on that night that I was able to put it together."

"Yet you still said nothing." Gwen leaned in. "You were a lonely, confused little boy, Ethan. Distressed about your mother's unhappiness and hurt by your father's distance. You misunderstood what you saw. Or maybe you had a dream and convinced yourself it was true in order to rationalize your negative feelings toward me."

"I didn't dream it."

"I remember that night well, too," Gwen said. "I came to your grandparents' home to confront your father about something he'd missed in the profile. He was already making mistakes. I was already seeing signs of his illness. But he never liked to be challenged, and we argued. It had nothing to do with an affair. Our relationship was never anything but professional."

"I know what I saw."

Gwen gave him a slight smile. "You sound so much like James right now. If I close my eyes, I could almost believe I'm sitting across the table from him, conversing the way we used to over a case. I never realized how much alike you are. So focused and single-minded. You don't like to be questioned or challenged, either, do you, Ethan?"

A warning thrill prickled his backbone. She'd laid a trap, and he'd willingly tripped the spring. Already, he could see the beginnings of the case to be made against him. If he overstepped his bounds in Charleston, if he dug up incriminating evidence that threatened the status quo, a subtle campaign would be initiated. This conversation was his warning. Next would come censure, suspension and then a career-killing transfer, if not outright termination, all accompanied by whispers of incompetence, insubordination and insanity.

As if intuiting his train of thought, Gwen said, "What else is on your mind, Ethan?"

"I think we're done."

"Yes, I agree. Time to call it a night. But it's been a most enlightening conversation," she said. "I feel better already now that we've cleared the air. One last thing, though. We still need to talk about Adaline Kinsella."

His gut tightened. "I don't see how she's any of your concern."

Gwen's brow creased as she reached for her jacket. "You caused a lot of trouble for that young woman ten years ago. You nearly derailed her career along with your own. I imagine you broke her heart in the process. I've spoken with Deputy Chief Cutler about my concerns."

"Concerns about me?"

"About Detective Kinsella. Did she tell you that she's been chosen by her department to attend my program? That's quite an honor. A real feather in her cap. But I won't waste my time on someone who isn't one hundred percent committed to the training. It wouldn't be fair to the other enrollees. Detective Kinsella is a promising candidate. She's a good cop—smart, diligent, ambitious. But I worry about outside distractions. It would be a shame if she lost focus and had to be cut from the current session."

Ethan tamped back his anger. "Is that a threat?"

"It's a warning. Leave her alone, Ethan. You screw this up for her, there won't be a second chance for either of you this time."

She stood, slipped on her jacket and left without a backward glance. Ethan paid the bill, and by the time he exited the coffee shop, she'd already crossed the street. The black Charger was nowhere to be seen. Instead, a gleaming Mercedes pulled to the curb, and Gwen got in the back.

Ethan watched as the car turned at the next intersection, and then he removed his cell phone from his pocket and checked his messages. He walked down the street until foot traffic died away. Pretending to tie his shoe, he hunkered at the curb and slipped his phone beneath the front tire of a parked cab.

Tomorrow he would buy a burner phone and turn in his rental car. Small measures that would inconvenience Gwen Holloway, but nothing would stop her once she set her sights on a target.

Chapter Six

The next morning, Addie sat in her parked car with a blueberry scone and iced coffee as she kept an eye on her surroundings. For someone who had a tendency to get bored and restless with too much time on her hands, she'd never minded surveillance. It gave her time to think, and she had plenty on her mind this morning.

Despite her insistence that sometimes a coincidence was just a coincidence, she wondered if the previous evening's events really could be connected to Ethan's arrival in Charleston. Maybe the trespasser hadn't been so much a prankster as a watcher. Someone sent to keep an eye on her. Rattle her cage with those flower petals.

Now she was starting to sound as paranoid and obsessed as Ethan.

Addie shivered despite the heat.

Her initial assumption about the interloper had likely been right. Even as a child, she'd known about that strange breed of spectators who tried to insinuate themselves into a tragedy, or worse, into a victim's life for self-aggrandizement. Her grandmother had tried to protect her from those who would cruelly invade their privacy, but from time to time a "fan" would slip through. Sometimes an aggressive reporter would ambush Addie on the playground or a photographer would hide in the bushes to try to get candid photographs for a story on Twilight's Children. Eventually the personal contact died away, and the letters that came later had never seemed threatening.

Someone creeping onto her property twenty-five years after her mother's death to scatter crimson magnolia petals along her walkway was a deeper kind of stalking. Not to mention the attack upon her person and the distorted murmur of her name, which had come back to haunt her in her sleep.

Addie had awakened in the middle of the night to that same electronic voice, only to realize she'd been dreaming. Unnerved by the nightmare, she'd gone all through the house, making sure nothing was amiss. The security system had still been activated, the doors locked tight, and yet Addie had had the strangest notion that someone had been in her house. Not possible, of course. She was a light sleeper. Even without the blare of an alarm, she would have awakened at the first sounds of an intruder. But that nagging feeling had kept her awake for the rest of the night, and now she struggled with heavy eyelids as the sun beat down through the windshield.

Taking another sip of the iced coffee, she idly tracked the pedestrian traffic as she rolled down the passenger window to get a cross breeze. Then she checked the rearview mirror as she adjusted her sunglasses. She felt confident she hadn't been followed. She knew how to spot and evade a tail. Still, recent events had left her edgy and overcautious. She kept her eyes peeled for a vehicle that made a second pass around the block or a tourist who lingered too long in front of a shop window.

A few minutes later, she spotted a familiar figure as he came around the corner on foot. He had his phone to his ear, walking briskly but not so fast as to attract attention. When he drew even with her car, she said through the open window, "Keep walking."

Ethan's hesitation was almost infinitesimal before he continued up the block and turned at the next intersection. Once she made sure *he* wasn't being followed, she got out of the car, locked the door and headed up the street behind him. He had already disappeared by the time she made the corner. She slowed her steps as if she were out for a morning stroll along the downtown streets.

A wrought iron gate across a narrow alleyway clanged in the breeze. Addie turned at the sound, and Ethan said from the shadows, "I'm in here."

His voice was deep, a little husky—perhaps

from his own sleepless night—and as mysterious as the gloom in which he hid. Addie could just make out his silhouette. Tall, lean, head slightly bowed as he observed her.

Watch your back, Addie. Maybe something darker rides along with him.

She suppressed another shiver as she glanced both ways down the street, telling herself she was still being cautious. She was just making sure no one had followed them, but her reaction to that voice, his nearness, the sight of him waiting for her in the shadows provoked an unexpected reaction. For a moment, ten years melted away and she felt hopelessly smitten and dangerously naive. At twenty-two, she hadn't stood a chance against Ethan Barrow's brooding intensity, but she was a decade older and, surely to goodness, wiser. She knew how to protect herself from men like Ethan and, more important, from her own weaknesses.

"Addie?"

"Give me a minute."

She wiped her hands down the sides of her jeans as she surveyed the traffic. It annoyed her that the mere sight of him could threaten her poise. That the sound of his voice could still catch her off guard. She found herself bombarded with images that were best left in the past. The way he'd looked at her, kissed her, the slow trace of his hands along her quivering body.

"What is it?" he demanded with soft urgency. "Were you followed?"

Addie beat back the images. "I don't think so," she said briskly. "But better safe than sorry." She took off her sunglasses as she stepped through the gate. After the glare of the sun, the deep shade of the alley momentarily blinded her.

Ethan straightened from the wall and came toward her. "Are you all right? What happened to your face?"

Her hand flew to her forehead. She'd forgotten about the bandage since changing it that morning after her shower. She was bruised, too, but the wounds were superficial. "There was an incident at my house last night. It's not important. I'm fine."

"What kind of incident?"

"We can talk about it later. That's not why I'm here."

"Then why are you here?" He searched her features. Her vision was still clouded, but for some reason, she had no trouble at all focusing on his eyes. They were dark and full of concern. "How did you know where to find me, anyway?"

"You aren't that hard to figure out." Her defensiveness made her sound petty, and she winced. She hated that tone. "Naomi Quinlan was killed at the next intersection, and she lived only a few blocks north of here. She would have walked this way to and from her home the night she died. I knew you'd come by sooner or later. I arrived early and waited."

"What makes you think I haven't already been by here?"

"Oh, I'm sure you have. Any number of times. And you'll keep coming back until you're satisfied you haven't missed something."

"That explains how you found me, but you still haven't told me why you're here."

She turned back into the sunlight. "I don't know, Ethan. I've been asking myself that same question for the better part of an hour. A part of me thinks that maybe I can keep you from doing something stupid, and another part of me thinks…" She trailed off. "I don't know what I think."

"Let me give it a go. You're here for the same reason I came back to Charleston." He leaned back against the building, seemingly relaxed, but Addie knew better. He was as anxious as she was about this meeting. "As much as you want to discount the possibility that I could be right, you can't. It's starting to eat at you. You're wondering if the person who murdered your mother could still be out there, and you can't stand the thought that the perpetrator has gotten away with it all these years. Maybe he's long gone or maybe he's still in the city. You're asking yourself, what if he kills again and you do nothing to stop him?"

His assessment was a little too spot-on, and that also annoyed her. "Are you profiling me?"

"You aren't that hard to figure out." Something close to tenderness took the sting out of his taunt. "Come away from the gate," he said. "It's better if we don't attract curious eyes." When she didn't budge, he pushed off the wall. "Addie."

"I heard you. I don't think we can be seen from the street."

Ethan was silent for a moment. "You're not afraid to be alone with me, are you?" His voice was steady, his tone nonjudgmental, but beneath his neutrality, something vulnerable lurked. An unsettling fusion of dread and need.

"If I were afraid, would I have met you last night? Would I have come looking for you this morning?"

His gaze burned into hers. "Maybe not. But sometime during the past ten years, the thought must have crossed your mind—like father, like son."

"I think you're capable of a lot of things, Ethan, but murder isn't one of them."

"Thank you for that."

"Don't thank me." She folded her arms. "I still don't trust you."

"And yet here you are."

She shook her head. "I must be out of my mind."

"Or maybe deep down, you realize that all I've ever wanted is the truth."

"You just didn't care who you took down in the process."

"I never meant to hurt you, Addie. I hope you know that."

She hardened her resolve against his regret. "What I know is that you have a history of deception, so I'll be watching you carefully. I'll take everything you tell me with a grain of salt. But you are right about one thing—I'm curious about that third DNA sample and the possibility of a donor match."

He nodded, his gaze going back to the cut on her forehead. "We can talk about Naomi Quinlan on the way to her house, but I'm not going anywhere until you tell me how you got hurt. Don't say it's not important. It is."

Addie's first inclination was to remind him that she wasn't his business, but all this blatant hostility was unproductive and it went against her nature. She didn't like clinging to her grudges. Her grandmother would be appalled at her comportment. *Be the better person, Addie. Life's too short. Don't let anger and bitterness steal your joy.*

Only her grandmother's memory could prod her into a truce with Ethan Barrow. She would let go of the bitterness, but her guard would remain up, Addie decided. Forgiving was one thing, forgetting quite another. "Someone came into my backyard last night. He was waiting for me when I got home. I gave chase and he ambushed me."

"You went after him alone?"

"I was armed and I wanted to frighten him enough so that he wouldn't be tempted to come back and do it again."

"Do what again?"

She paused. "He scattered crimson magnolia petals on my walkway."

She could sense Ethan's heightened tension even though his expression remained neutral. "When was this?"

"Right after I left you, I found a trail from the garage to my back door. And then I spotted him—or someone—hiding in the shadows near the fence. I figure he'd waited there to witness my reaction. I pursued him through a couple of yards into a gutted house. I let down my guard, and he hit me with a board so that he could get away." She touched the bandage again. "It's not serious. Barely more than a scratch. My ego took a worse beating. I should never have let him get the drop on me. I'm not usually so careless."

"Did you call it in?"

"I called Matt Lepear. He came over, and we both searched the property and the surrounding area, but the suspect was long gone. It's like I told you yesterday. All the publicity surrounding the anniversary is bringing out the crazies."

Ethan wasn't buying her explanation. "This wasn't just a prank. You were assaulted."

"I'll be more careful in the future."

Now it was his turn to glance both ways down the street. "We both need to be more careful. I appreciate that you came here looking for me this morning, but it's probably not a good idea for us to be seen together."

"Why? What happened?"

His gaze whipped back to hers. "I also had a run-in last night. Gwen Holloway was waiting for me when I got back to my hotel."

"*The* Gwen Holloway. What did she want?"

"That's a good question. Gwen says one thing but often means another. She *says* my trip to Charleston has her concerned and, apparently, others are worried as well. According to Gwen, powerful people are keeping tabs on me, one of them possibly my stepfather."

Addie looked at him in alarm. "Why would your stepfather spy on you?"

Ethan shrugged. "To protect his image. He holds an important position in the DOJ. Maybe he's afraid I'll step out of line and embarrass him the way I did ten years ago."

"Seems a bit extreme. Could he have another motive?"

"Unlikely. He wasn't around for the Twilight Killer case or for my father's incarceration. They knew each other, but Richard didn't come into the picture until later. I'd be more inclined to think that Gwen is somehow manipulating him to try to control me."

Addie gave him a look. "That sounds a little paranoid, even for you."

"I know how it sounds. I also know Gwen Holloway has a lot to lose if that third DNA sample pans out. Her whole career was built on my father's downfall. Respect and reputation mean everything to her. Which brings me to another problem. Why didn't you tell me you've been accepted into her program?"

"I didn't think it mattered. And why is it a problem?"

"She's threatening to cut you loose if I don't drop my investigation."

"She said that?" Addie muttered an expletive that drew an amused glance from Ethan. "Sorry for the language, but the idea that she would even try something like that just pisses me off. I'll tell her to her face what she can do with her program."

Ethan's eyes glinted. "As much as I would pay to see that confrontation, don't give her the ammunition. And don't throw away an important opportunity for pride's sake. You can learn to manipulate her."

"How?"

"There are two kinds of people she routinely drops from her program. Those who can't cut it and those who set out to prove they're smarter than she is. You're smart, but you're also clever. You can make her look good without showing her up. She'll respect that."

"How do you know so much about Gwen Holloway?" Addie asked.

"She's pushed my buttons a few too many times. I've learned from my mistakes. If you can keep your cool, she's not that hard to figure out, either."

"Good to know." Addie slipped her sunglasses back on. "Should we go take a look at the crime scene? Maybe I'll remember something about that night that we can use."

He looked uneasy. "I know I brought all this to your doorstep, but you don't have to get involved. Things didn't go well for either of us last time, and now you have more to lose."

"Things went south because you lied to me," Addie said. "You didn't even tell me your real name until I was in too deep. Do you have any idea how much that hurt? How humiliating it was to find out who you really are and what you really wanted from me?"

"Addie—"

"Do you seriously think a career is the worst thing a person can lose?"

"Addie."

"Stop saying my name."

"I don't know what else to say. I should have been straight with you from the start. But before I could come clean, I was in too deep, too. I fell for you and then I didn't want you to know the truth."

She looked at the sidewalk, the traffic, anywhere but at him. Anger blossomed, but she pressed it back down. Ten years was a long time to carry the weight of a broken heart. She was fine now. She'd been fine for a very long time. Best to let go of all that negative energy. It would only trip her up. She'd come here to find Ethan of her own accord. No one had twisted her arm. Either she was going to help him get at the truth or she wasn't. No need to keep punishing him for something that was over and done with. Neither of them could change the past.

"Let's just get on with this," she said. "What happened, happened. We're both adults. Let's put it behind us and move on."

"You mean that?"

"I do. But there's something you need to know. It's true I'm curious about that third DNA sample and the possibility of a donor match, and you've raised valid concerns about the hit-and-run that took Naomi Quinlan's life. It does seem a little too convenient. I also don't like being threatened by Gwen Holloway or anyone else, and I'm starting to wonder if she had something to do with what happened at my house last night." Addie held up her hand when Ethan tried to interrupt. "Having said all that, I still think my mother's killer is exactly where he belongs. I still think justice was served twenty-five years ago. But on the slight chance I could be wrong...well, that's why I'm here. That's the *only* reason I'm here."

ADDIE WAS QUIET as they walked along the tree-lined street, and Ethan didn't try to initiate conversation. She appeared deep in thought, and he didn't want to annoy her. She seemed to have a short fuse these days. He could understand that, and he'd gladly give her a pass. Considering everything that had gone down between them, her willingness to put the past behind them was a gracious olive branch.

Addie's interest in the case encouraged him—two pairs of eyes were always better than one when searching for the truth—but he still worried about the consequences of her involvement. Gwen Holloway could cause a lot of trouble for both of them, and Ethan knew only too well that she could be vindictive. She'd already gone to the deputy chief with her concerns, putting Addie in the crosshairs. But Gwen may have underestimated her opponent. Addie was no pushover. She'd made it clear she wouldn't allow anyone to intimidate or manipulate her, and that included Ethan. He respected that. He admired her willingness to fight back. As for him, he would never try to deceive her again. He'd learned his lesson ten years ago. From now on, total honesty. That was the only way their new alliance would work.

He decided it was time to break the awkward silence. "Must be getting close to ninety out here. It's too early to be this hot. Not much of a breeze, either."

Addie gave him a sidelong glance. "Maybe you're too used to sitting in an air-conditioned office. You ought to try walking a beat."

"Detectives don't walk beats, either."

"No, but we canvass," she said. "And before I made detective, I walked my share of foot patrols. You get used to the heat."

She certainly looked cool and relaxed in a white tank, jeans and sockless sneakers. She'd pulled her hair back in a ponytail, and he could see a faint sheen of lip gloss when the sun hit her just right. She smelled good, too, like fresh air and flowers, a clean scent that emanated from her skin and hair when she moved in close. Even off duty and dressed so casually, she exuded confidence and control. She walked along the street, head up, eyes alert, ready to take on the world. He had no doubt she was carrying. The cross-body bag was less conspicuous than a holster and would also contain her keys and cell phone. Ethan was likewise armed, the weapon tucked up under his shirt in the back.

He glanced over his shoulder as they made the next corner. It was still early. The shops hadn't yet opened, and few people were stirring. The sparse traffic would make it easy to spot the black Charger or any other suspicious vehicle.

"Relax," Addie said. "We're not being followed. We would have spotted a tail by now."

"Weren't you the one who just said better safe than sorry?"

"There's careful and there's paranoid." Addie nodded toward a side street. "Naomi's house is just down that way."

"Yes, I know. It's the white one-story on the left."

Addie glanced at him but said nothing. She had been right, of course. He'd already been by Naomi Quinlan's house once and walked the crime scene twice, and he would keep coming back until he had his answers.

The cottage was protected from the street by a fence and a garden of tropical foliage. Morning glories wound around the wrought iron posts and Ethan could smell jasmine, a scent he would always associate with Charleston even though the vine was not uncommon in Prince William County, Virginia, where he now lived.

"Maybe we should have come in the back way," he said. "There's an alley that runs behind the house."

"The problem with coming in through the back is that if you're seen by the neighbors, you look mighty suspicious. Someone could call the police. Or worse, shoot you."

"We could always come back after dark," he suggested.

"And then what? We just break in?"

"What did you think we were going to do?"

Even from behind her sunglasses, he could feel the power of her focus. "I don't know, Ethan. I guess I'm just trying to convince myself there's a line I still won't cross."

...t got to him. It brought home all over again what she had risked for him in the past and what he was asking of her now. "Go back to your car," he said. "I'll handle things here."

"Too late. We've been spotted." Addie gave a slight nod to the house next door.

Ethan's gaze swept the neighbor's garden until he spotted an older woman kneeling in front of a flower bed. She was nearly hidden by a thick hedge of rosebushes, but he had no doubt she was thoroughly checking them out beneath the wide brim of her straw hat. After another moment of covert observation, she stood, peeled off her gloves and came over to the fence to call out to them.

"Excuse me! Are you looking for Naomi? I'm afraid she isn't home."

"We were just looking at the house," Ethan said as he shot Addie a glance. They walked down the sidewalk to the neighbor's yard. She came through the gate to meet them, pausing to brush off the knees of her work pants.

"Did one of the agencies send you over? I'm surprised they're showing the place so soon. Naomi's barely cold, poor thing, and no one's been by to clean out her things. But I retired from real estate years ago. Business is done differently these days, I expect." She pushed off her hat, letting it hang down her back by the chin strap. Her face was round and flushed, her eyes beady and avid. "You heard about the accident, no doubt."

"Yes."

"Such a tragedy for someone so young." The woman's birdlike gaze vectored in on Ethan.

"You knew her well?" he asked.

"I don't know about well, but we were neighbors and I suppose you could say we were friends. I sold her aunt this house years ago, along with a number of rental properties all over the city. But that's neither here nor there. I'm Ida McFall, by the way. I've been keeping an eye on the place ever since the accident. One can't be too careful these days."

"That's smart," Ethan said.

Her head tilted slightly, and the beady eyes deepened with suspicion. "I didn't catch your name."

"Ethan Barrow." He held up his credentials. "I'm with the FBI. This is Detective Kinsella with the Charleston PD."

Ethan didn't know what he had expected in the way of a reaction. A badge and credentials often put people on the defensive even when they had nothing to hide. But Ida McFall's face instantly transformed. Her wariness faded, replaced by a of genuine incredulity. "Oh, my word, you're *him*, aren't you?"

"I beg your pardon?"

"Naomi's FBI agent." She took off her hat and fanned herself for a moment. "Forgive me, but this is a bit overwhelming. She spoke of you in such glowing terms that I wondered if she'd made you up, especially when you were so conspicuously absent after her death. I'm sorry I doubted you. I blame Naomi's wild imagination and her tendency to exaggerate. Sometimes I couldn't tell her fantasy life from her reality. Writers." She shook her head.

"Naomi told me she was a genealogist."

"She taught genealogy at the community college, but her passion was writing. She gave me the impression you were working on a project together. She implied the two of you had become close." Ida McFall's expression turned coy. "She was certainly taken with you, Agent Barrow, and I can see why."

Ethan exchanged another glance with Addie, who lifted a brow. She had pushed her sunglasses to the top of her head, and even though her expression remained composed, he had an inkling of her thoughts. Had a woman with a secret, perhaps even a fantastical agenda, baited him into coming to Charleston? Was his search for the DNA match nothing more than a wild-goose chase?

"I think you've misconstrued our relationship," he told Ida. "I barely knew Naomi Quinlan."

"And yet here you are," she said. "You came, exactly as Naomi predicted you would. And if she was right about you, I have to believe the other things she told me were true as well."

"What other things?"

"That she was in danger. That powerful people were out to get her because of damaging evidence she'd dug up. She warned me that she was being followed. She said someone watched her house at night, but I thought she was imagining things. I never saw anything suspicious. Even after I learned of her death, I tried to tell myself it was just an accident. Naomi's head was always in the clouds. Perhaps she was distracted that night and didn't see the car coming. Now I know the danger was real. Naomi was murdered. The driver of that car deliberately ran her down. Thank God you've come, Agent Barrow. Someone has to get to the bottom of that poor girl's death."

"I'm sure the police are doing everything they can to find the driver," Addie said.

"I wish I shared your confidence."

"Meaning?"

"It's been two weeks, and as far as I can tell, nothing has been done about Naomi's case. Either she isn't a priority to the Charleston Police Department or something fishy is going on."

"Fishy how?"

"You tell me… Detective Kinsella, was it?"

A frown flitted across Addie's brow at the woman's disapproving tone, but she didn't rise to the bait.

"Detective Kinsella and I will do everything we can to find out what happened to Naomi, but we'll need your help," Ethan said. "Anything you can tell us could be useful. Please don't hold back. Despite what you seem to think, I know virtually nothing about her life. We exchanged a handful of emails, and that was the extent of our interaction."

Ida's assumptions remained steadfast. "Sometimes the most powerful connections are forged through the written word. I corresponded for years with a man I never met. Over time, we developed a bond that became unbreakable. I only mention that relationship because his letters to me inspired Naomi's book. I can't help wondering if there's a connection to her murder."

"What was his name?" Addie asked, with an odd note in her voice.

The older woman's chin came up in defiance. "Orson Lee Finch. Yes, *that* Orson Lee Finch. We shared a love of gardening and rare plants, and I make no apology for our friendship. Mr. Finch was a kind, thoughtful, *gentle* man, and quite refined for someone in his circumstances. I don't

Chapter Seven

Ida McFall's association with the notorious serial killer caught Ethan by surprise, but judging
by Addie's satisfied nod, she had already intuited
the identity of the woman's pen pal. Ethan gave
an answering nod, indicating that she should take
the lead while he remained silent. He might feel
compelled to defend his father, and the last thing
he wanted was to stifle Ida McFall's candor.

He studied the woman surreptitiously while
Addie questioned her. Apparently, Naomi had ne-
glected to tell Ida of Ethan's relationship to James
Merrick, and he had to wonder if there was a reason for that.

"Do you still have Finch's letters?" Addie asked.

"I gave them to Naomi. I suspect she hid them
somewhere in her office, along with all her notes.
She wasn't just frightened for her safety. She was
paranoid someone might try to steal her work.
Dozens of books have been written about the Twilight Killer and his nemesis, James Merrick, but

Naomi was certain her new evidence would give the story a twist."

"Did she tell you the nature of this new evidence?"

"Only that she suspected the police had been involved in covering it up."

Addie's voice sharpened. "Covering it up how?"

"I don't know. She never gave me the details. But I know she didn't trust the police. With good reason, it seems."

Addie ignored the inference. "Did she name names?"

"No, but a detective came around asking questions a few days after Naomi's death. He was courteous enough, but there was something about him that made me uneasy." Ida paused thoughtfully. "I couldn't put my finger on it, exactly. All I know is that my instincts are rarely wrong. I think he may have been looking for Naomi's evidence. I'm certain he was fishing for something. He said he would be in touch, but I never heard back from him."

"Did he tell you his name, show you his identification?" Addie asked.

"I remember he had a badge. He was an older gentleman. Around my age, I would guess. Well dressed and handsome with salt-and-pepper hair. He wore those mirrored sunglasses that made him look like a pilot."

"But you didn't catch his name?"

"If he said, I've forgotten. He didn't stay long. He claimed his visit was just a routine follow-up. Wanted to know if anyone had been in and out of Naomi's house. I told him no, not that I'd seen."

"You said Naomi was worried about someone stealing her work," Addie said. "Was there anyone in particular that concerned her?"

"Besides the police? Her aunt, Vivian Du-Priest."

Addie looked taken aback. "Wait. Do you mean Vivian DuPriest, the author?"

"Yes, she's the one. Do you know her work?"

"Not personally, but when I was a kid, my grandmother used to read all her books." Addie turned to Ethan. "Years ago she worked the crime beat for the paper, but she was better known for her true-crime page-turners."

"She was very successful," Ida said. "Not that the DuPriests have ever wanted for money. Naomi came from the poor side of the family. Vivian took her in after her parents died and gave her a job as her assistant. Mostly she ran errands. But they had a falling-out sometime back."

"What about?" Addie asked.

"Vivian accused Naomi of trying to ride her coattails to fame and fortune, but I think she was secretly afraid someone younger and more ambitious would overshadow her. Vivian always had a bigger-than-life persona to go with her outsize ego, but after the incident, she wasn't able to produce, and her readers eventually abandoned her. She became a recluse, seemingly content to live off her past glories—until Naomi started to write. That's when the trouble started. There was an ugly dustup, and Vivian kicked the girl out."

"How did she end up next door to you?"

"As I said, Vivian owns the house. Setting her niece up in one of her rentals probably helped assuage her conscience."

"You sound as if you know Vivian DuPriest pretty well," Addie said.

Ida shrugged. "Not that well, but I met her long before I knew Naomi. Vivian is the one who introduced me to Mr. Finch."

"How did that come about?"

"It was happenstance, really. I had an elderly relative who lived across the street from the Du-Priest home. When he fell ill, I used to help care for his garden on weekends. Vivian would sometimes stop by to chat about the plants. I was having trouble with the gardenias, and she told me I should write to Mr. Finch and ask for his advice."

Addie glanced at Ethan. "You didn't think that an odd suggestion?"

"I was stunned at first. I could hardly imagine such a thing. But Vivian had been to the prison to speak with him, and she was impressed by his intelligence. Perhaps *intrigued* is a better word. Whether she believed him guilty or not, I couldn't say. She was quite cagey in that regard. After a while, I became excited about the notion of a secret pen pal, and so I sent off a letter before I could change my mind. He answered right away."

"Did you ever go see him in person?"

"No, I never did." She sighed. "I suppose I didn't want the reality of his situation to interfere with our friendship."

Addie flashed Ethan another glance, and he nodded that she should continue. "Did you share the letters with Vivian?"

"At first. Then her parsing became too intrusive. She wanted to dissect his every word."

"But you gave the letters to Naomi."

"By then a lot of time had passed. I was no longer as emotionally connected to our correspondence as I once was."

Ethan had remained quiet for the exchange, but now he said, "You mentioned an incident. What happened to Vivian DuPriest that she was no longer able to write?"

"It was her habit to go out walking alone at night. She called it her thinking time. Someone attacked her near her home and left her for dead. She had a long and painful recovery, both mentally and physically. The assault changed her whole personality. She rarely left her house and was never able to write again. Her last book remains unfinished to this day."

"Was she writing about Orson Lee Finch?" Addie asked.

"About the Twilight Killer case, yes. How did you know?"

"Just a guess."

Ida lowered her voice as she glanced across the garden to Naomi's house. "Do you think there could be a connection between her attack and the hit-and-run that killed Naomi?"

"As you said, a lot of time has passed," Ethan hedged. "Did Naomi have many visitors? Did she ever mention having problems with anyone?"

"Aside from Vivian? She mostly kept to herself."

"What about a boyfriend?"

"No one serious. No one that I knew of, at least."

"Do you think her aunt would allow us inside the house to have a look around?"

"No need to bother Vivian. I can let you in. Naomi gave me a spare key so that I could feed her cat while she was away. Take as much time as you need. All I ask is that you leave everything as you found it. The idea of strangers invading Naomi's privacy makes me uncomfortable." She paused with a smile. "But I don't think she'd mind you going through her things, Agent Barrow."

"TALK ABOUT A TWIST," Addie said as they stepped inside Naomi's foyer.

"The pen pal thing? I didn't see that coming." Ethan closed the front door and took a quick survey of their surroundings. It was an older home, with long windows and walled-off spaces. The foyer led directly into the living area, and through open doorways he glimpsed the dining room and kitchen. The bedrooms would be off the narrow hallway to the left. From what he could see, the furnishings were sparse and serviceable. That was good. The lack of clutter would make their search easier.

He filed away his impressions and turned to glance out the front window. Ida McFall dawdled at the garden gate, staring back at the house. She had her phone to her ear, but the brim of her hat obscured her expression. There was something about her demeanor that niggled. Ethan couldn't shake the notion that the woman wasn't as helpful as she wanted them to think. Like everyone else he had spoken to lately, Ida McFall might have her own agenda.

Addie came up beside him at the window. "Who do you suppose she's talking to?"

"No clue."

"What do you make of her, anyway?" she mused. "She sure was chatty."

"Maybe a little too chatty," Ethan said.

"My thoughts exactly. But it could be a simple case of nerves. People react differently to law enforcement. Some clam up, while others can't spill their guts fast enough. And people her age sometimes get lonely. All they want is a captive audience and a sympathetic ear."

"That's a generous assessment considering her attitude toward cops."

Addie shrugged. "If I took offense every time someone disparaged my job, I wouldn't be able to get out of bed in the mornings." Her gaze narrowed as she stared out the window. "I have to say, though, it does seem awfully convenient that Naomi Quinlan's next-door neighbor once had a direct line of communication to Orson Lee Finch."

"Not really a coincidence if her letters were the inspiration for Naomi's book. Sounds like all three women had a connection to Finch."

Addie folded her arms. "About that book. She never mentioned to you that she was writing about Finch or your father?"

"Not once. She always presented herself as a genealogist."

"Would it have changed anything had you known? Would it have made you more suspect of her motives?"

Ethan thought about that for a minute. "Probably. But I would have come, anyway."

Addie nodded. "I figured."

"Does it change anything for you?" he asked.

She gave his query the same consideration. "Not really. Because no matter what her motive was in contacting you, we're still looking for the same thing."

"The truth?"

"The truth, yes, but more specifically, that DNA match. If it exists." She turned back to the foyer. "Where do you want to start?"

"We should split up to cover more ground. If Naomi went to the trouble of hiding Finch's letters and her notes, we can assume she concealed the DNA results as well. My hunch is, she put everything on a thumb drive."

"The proverbial needle in a haystack then." Addie moved to the glass door to the right of the foyer. "I'll start in her office. You can search her bedroom, seeing as how she wouldn't have minded you going through her things." Her blue eyes glinted as she glanced over her shoulder. "What was the word Ida used? *Taken.* Naomi was *taken* with you. Those emails must have really been something."

He gave her a warning look. "You just couldn't help yourself, could you?"

"Sadly, no. But don't begrudge me. I've waited a long time for this."

"I can tell."

The banter helped relieve a lingering tension, but Ethan reminded himself that one playful moment meant nothing. A few throwaway lines didn't erase years of anger and resentment. Still, he hadn't seen Addie so unguarded since his return, and his mind wandered into places he had no business going. They had always worked well together whether she wanted to admit it or not. It was their personal relationship that had come undone. What would their lives be like now if things had gone differently ten years ago? If he had been honest with her from the start? Would they still be together, married maybe, with a kid or two?

Funny that he should even have such a thought. Ethan had never considered himself a family man. He was too much of a loner, too intensely focused on his career and in righting the wrongs of the past. Now he felt keenly the loss of something that was never meant to be. He carried too much baggage to ever have a chance with Addie again. He accepted the inevitable, but the thought of missing that smile every morning for the rest his life was a pain that had started to gnaw at his soul.

"Ethan? Did you hear me?"

He pulled himself out of his reverie. "I'm sorry?"

She gave him a curious glance. "I said holler if you find anything." She handed him a pair of disposable gloves from her bag.

He snapped them on as she opened the office door. She stopped short, stared into the room for a moment and then said, "Looks like someone beat us to the punch."

He followed her into the office, and they both stood gazing around. The room had apparently been tossed and put back together in haste. Desk drawers were only partially closed, and books had been haphazardly returned to the shelves. A corner of the rug had been turned back. A piece of artwork hung askew.

"There's no computer," Ethan said as he walked over to the desk. "Unusual for a writer. Unless someone took her laptop." He opened drawers, searched through the contents and then checked for false bottoms.

"Maybe she had it with her the night she was hit. I can check the list of personal effects when I go back to HQ." Addie moved around the room, peering behind paintings and underneath seat cushions. "Do you know if she told anyone else about her DNA database searches?"

"I doubt she did. She seemed extremely cautious and secretive about what she'd found. But she also never mentioned that her aunt was the reporter assigned to my father's case or that her neighbor once wrote love letters to Orson Lee Finch."

"Maybe she didn't *tell* anyone. Maybe she started asking questions and someone took notice of her interest. Hold that thought." Addie left the room and came back a few minutes later. "No sign of a forced entry front or back. Both doors have dead bolts, and the windows in the rear have burglar bars. Whoever searched this office likely had a key. Or else Ida let someone else in."

Ethan hunkered down and looked underneath the desk, then ran his hand all along the bottom.

"Maybe the driver removed Naomi's key from her body before he fled the scene."

"He could have taken her laptop, too." Addie sifted through the contents of the bookshelves. "The owner of the house would also have a key, wouldn't she? Maybe we should pay Vivian Du-Priest a visit. If she'll see us, that is."

"Oh, I'm pretty sure she'll see us," Ethan said. "I'm James Merrick's son and you're the daughter of his victim. She won't be able to resist."

"One way to find out."

"Agreed." Ethan walked across the floor, testing for loose boards.

"I find it curious that Naomi kept all her aunt's bestsellers on display even though they had a falling-out. Most of them are autographed, too. *To Naomi with greatest affection.* She even has a picture of the two of them together. They looked pretty chummy when this shot was taken." Addie studied the photograph. "She was pretty. Naomi. I couldn't tell much about her appearance that night on the street."

Ethan understood the insinuation. A moving vehicle could do a lot of damage to the human body. He came over to check out the photograph. "I see now why Ida said Vivian DuPriest had a larger-than-life personality. I don't think I've ever met anyone with hair quite that shade of red."

"She was always something of a character, the

best I remember. A bohemian socialite, if there is such a thing. A local celebrity, for sure. Used to make all the morning talk-show rounds." Addie returned the frame to the shelf. "You never answered Ida when she asked if you thought there could be a connection between Naomi's death and Vivian's attack."

"You may not like what I think."

Addie shrugged. "Let's hear it."

"Crime-beat reporters cultivate sources in police departments. If someone leaked information about a cover-up to Vivian, she could have become a target."

Addie looked annoyed. "Nice theory, but no one has yet explained what this alleged cover-up entailed."

"I keep coming back to Naomi's last email," Ethan said. "She seemed certain the results of her DNA search could damage reputations."

"Like Gwen Holloway's."

He eyed her uneasily. "Gwen Holloway wasn't the only one who built a career on my father's case. David Cutler became a local hero after he made the arrest."

Addie's irritation quickened. "But unlike Gwen Holloway, he never cashed in on his notoriety. He stayed on the force as a detective and worked his way up through the ranks. He earned every promotion he got the hard way, and there is no one in the department with more integrity."

"People make mistakes. Even David Cutler. I know you consider him family, but no one's infallible."

Her eyes glittered a warning. "David Cutler's reputation isn't up for debate or discussion. Let's just get on with the search."

So much for an open mind, Ethan thought. He wasn't as convinced of the deputy chief's unimpeachable honor as she was, but for now he let the matter drop. Their alliance was still too tenuous to test the boundaries.

A car door sounded, and Addie went over to the window to glance out. "We've got company."

Ethan moved up beside her. A patrol car had pulled up to the curb directly in front of the house. Two uniformed officers got out and converged on the sidewalk outside the gate.

"What are they doing here?" Addie muttered. "Do you think Ida ratted us out?"

"I think we shouldn't stick around to find out." Ethan cast a glance around the room to make sure they hadn't left a trace of their visit. "Come on, let's go."

Addie was still at the window watching the officers. "We can't just run from the police. How do you think it'll look if Ida mentions my name? Maybe I should go out there and talk to them."

"And say what? We don't have a plausible excuse for being inside Naomi Quinlan's house unless you tell them about the DNA results. And that would open a can of worms I'd rather you not have to deal with. It's best if we avoid a confrontation."

"You're forgetting that I have a vested interest in Naomi's case. I was at the scene the night she died," Addie said. "I could say I'm here on a follow-up, which I am, in a way."

"Is that a story you really want to try to sell to the deputy chief? Why borrow trouble?" He took her arm. "Let's just get out of here."

She turned with a reluctant nod and followed him through the house to a small sun porch at the back. She went out first and paused on the steps to glance around while Ethan locked the door with Ida's key. Then she nodded an all clear.

They hurried through the garden in a half crouch, using the back gate to escape from the premises. A dog barked from one of the enclosed yards as they jogged down the alley away from Naomi's house. When they came to the end, they slowed to a walk and crossed the street, taking refuge behind the wrought iron gates of one the city's oldest churchyards. No one was about, but the bells that tolled from the belfry seemed ominous.

"Do you think we were spotted?" Addie asked.

"No, we're good for now."

"I don't know if I would put it that optimistically. We did just run from the police."

"We avoided unnecessary contact."

She tucked back her hair. "You really are

good with semantics, aren't you? Not to mention justification."

"Addie—"

She lifted her hand to silence his protest. "I know. No one twisted my arm."

He watched her for a moment. "We didn't break any laws."

"Not yet. But you've only been in town a couple of days. Give it time." There was no humor in her voice now. Not the slightest hint of her earlier teasing.

She stepped back into the shade, taking a moment to cool down and catch her breath. The light slanting down through the trees picked up the gold flecks in her blue eyes. Her lips were slightly parted as she stared up at him, and for a moment, Ethan had to fight the urge to weave his fingers through her hair, pull her close and kiss her as he'd wanted to do since their first meeting at the Gainey house.

Had that only been yesterday? Seemed like a lifetime ago, and yet in some ways, it felt as if they'd never been apart. Same old arguments. Same intense attraction. Memories flooded Ethan's head. Desire clouded his good sense. Before he could stop himself, he lifted a hand to smooth back her hair.

She caught her breath at his touch.

"Addie." He murmured her name as he wound a soft tendril around his finger.

Sunlight danced like fire in her eyes. "You keep saying my name as if you expect me to just fall back under your spell. It won't work, Ethan. You and I are not going to happen. We've established a temporary truce, but I still don't trust you. You're on a mission and I know how you get when you're obsessed. Nothing else matters. Not food, not sleep. Not even the law."

"At least you didn't say sex."

She rolled her eyes. "Oh, sex always mattered to you."

"And to you."

Their glazes clung for a moment, his hot and testing, hers fierce and defiant. He could see her now the way she'd looked at twenty-two. Naked in the moonlight as she ran toward the sea. Proudly uninhibited and breathtakingly beautiful. *Come in with me, Ethan. The water feels like silk.* Her skin wet, warm to his touch. Her legs wrapped around him as the waves gently rocked them.

His pulse thudded at the memory. "Is it so inconceivable that I might have changed in ten years?"

"We've both changed, Ethan. And yet here we are, right back where we left off. Running away from the police. Sneaking into places we have no business. Crossing fine lines. Risking everything for a case that was closed twenty-five years ago. I don't blame you for any of that. You've made no pretense about your intentions. This time, it's all on me. My choices, my consequences." She moved up to the entrance, surveying the street before she turned back to him. "Did you ever ask yourself why we bring out the worst in each other? That maybe, just maybe, what happened to my mother at the hands of your father is a barrier too high for us to scale? That maybe we shouldn't even try?"

"All the time," he said softly.

He saw a shiver go through her as she wrapped her arms around her middle. Defensive. Uncertain. And angry with herself for feeling that way.

"Addie…"

"Say my name like that one more time and I swear—"

He held up a hand to cut her off as the rumble of a powerful engine sounded nearby. He took a position on the opposite side of the gates.

"False alarm," he said.

"We should get moving."

"Not yet. If anyone comes looking for us, we'll be harder to spot in here than out on the street."

Her eyes glittered with frustration. "Who would come looking for us, Ethan?"

"I told you earlier, Gwen Holloway is already gunning for us both."

"You seriously think she would hunt us down on the street?"

His voice hardened. "She would do that and

more if she considered either of us a threat. You need to at least trust me on that."

"Still a tall order," Addie said bluntly. "Are you sure you've told me everything?"

"You know as much as I do."

She paused as another car went by. She tracked the blue sedan until it turned at the next corner. "Now you've got me acting all paranoid."

"You know what they say. It's not paranoid if someone is really out to get you."

Addie returned her focus to the street. She kept watch in one direction, Ethan the other. "You think Gwen had us followed to Naomi's and then called the police on us? Why would she do that?"

"To get us out of the house would be my guess."

Addie pondered that scenario for a moment. "For the sake of argument, let's assume Gwen is behind everything. Let's say she sent someone to search Naomi's office to look for the DNA results. If she or her people called the cops to get us out of the house, then that likely means they didn't find what they were looking for." She spoke in a low, pensive tone, and Ethan didn't interrupt her. He kept his gaze peeled while she sifted through her thoughts. "From everything I know about Gwen Holloway, she's methodical and meticulous and she demands the same of her subordinates. How does that square with the sloppy search of Naomi's office?"

"They were in a hurry. They got interrupted."

"By us?" That possibility seemed to unnerve her. She glanced around anxiously. "We can't hide in here forever. Let's just go back to my car."

"You're right," he said. "You should go."

"What about you?"

"I'd like another crack at finding that thumb drive."

Addie stared at him in alarm. "You don't even know you're looking for a thumb drive. Those DNA results could be hidden anywhere. And if Gwen is as dangerous and desperate as you seem to think, she's bound to have someone watching the house. She won't risk letting you inside again."

"I'll be fine. Go out the main entrance of the churchyard and keep to the alleys as much as you can. You should be able to make it to your vehicle undetected."

Addie's chin came up. "Don't worry about me. I know all about the secret backstreets in this city."

He nodded. "I'm sure you do, but be careful anyway, okay?"

The fire seemed to drain out of her then. She held his gaze for the longest moment before glancing away. "You're the one who needs to be careful. Trouble always follows wherever you go."

"This is a dangerous time for both of us," he said. "We're shaking things up while we're still in the dark. We don't yet know who all the bad actors are."

Addie gave him a sidelong glance. "It's always dangerous when you don't know who you can trust."

"I trust you."

She fell silent. "Maybe you shouldn't. I'm not as committed to this as you are. I have my own responsibilities and my own loyalties."

"Even so, you still came looking for me this morning."

"Don't read too much into that," she warned. "I'm only here because I want to put the past to rest for both of us. But you should know that if push comes to shove, I intend to protect myself this time."

"I wouldn't have it any other way."

Still she lingered, her gaze dark and watchful. "Ethan?"

"What is it, Addie?"

"You shouldn't have come back."

"Are you sorry I did?"

She closed her eyes on a deep sigh. "No. And that worries me most of all."

He leaned back against the wall and watched her stride away, ponytail swinging, hips subtly swaying. Ethan had always admired her walk. Not cocky, not coy, just straight-up confident.

He reluctantly turned away, moving through the gates and onto the sidewalk. The morning light hit him in the eyes, and he slipped his sunglasses back on, taking note of his surroundings—delivery trucks, parked cars, nearby businesses. A man crossing the street.

Other than the one lone pedestrian, the area was quiet. Too quiet. The calm before the storm, Ethan thought as he headed back to Naomi Quinlan's house.

Chapter Eight

Addie berated herself as she made her way across the churchyard, resisting the urge to glance over her shoulder to see if Ethan watched her. She'd felt his gaze on her back when she walked away, but maybe that had only been her imagination. Maybe the dark heat in his eyes and that knowing smile had only been wishful thinking.

Addie, Addie, what are you doing?

Was she really going down this road again when her future in the department had never looked brighter? Was she once more willing to risk it all because she couldn't smother the embers of an old attraction?

Ten years. *Ten years* and she still hadn't gotten Ethan Barrow out of her system. What was it about him that could tie her in knots with nothing more than a fleeting smile or a lingering stare? Addie had convinced herself she was smarter than that. Tougher than that. *And yet here you are.*

She shook off her doom and gloom as she left the churchyard and walked two blocks before ducking into another alley. She had other things to focus on at the moment. Like Naomi Quinlan's hit-and-run. Like a possible match to the third DNA sample found at her mother's murder scene.

Addie had just turned seven when Sandra Kinsella had been killed. Some days, she could barely recall what her mother looked like, and then there were times, especially in the dead of night when she lay awake staring at the ceiling, that she not only remembered her mother's features, but the scent of her perfume and the deep red of her favorite lipstick. Addie had bought that same classic shade for herself, though she rarely wore it. The color reminded her too much of a crimson magnolia.

Besides, red lipstick didn't really suit her. She wasn't her mother's daughter. Sandra Kinsella had been capricious and bold, a woman who gleefully embraced her darkest emotions and deepest desires. Addie wasn't like that. She was cautious and serious. Or at least…she had been until Ethan Barrow had come into her life.

Him again.

Addie frowned.

Put him out of your mind and focus.

Her mother's face wasn't the one she saw now in the back of her mind, nor was it her mother's whiskey-smooth voice she heard in her ear. The imagined reproach came from Helen Cutler, a woman who had been there for Addie through thick and thin, who had been both confidante and guardian. Helen had encouraged Addie to reach for the stars even as David Cutler had held her feet to the ground.

Was it at all conceivable that the deputy chief had been involved in a police cover-up twenty-five years ago, one involving her mother's murder and that third DNA sample? Addie didn't think such a thing possible. David Cutler was as straight an arrow as one could find in the police department, and he'd earned the respect and admiration of every man and woman who served under his command. And yet his promotion had allowed him to seal some of her mother's case files that remained out of Addie's reach to this day. She hadn't questioned his action, because she thought she knew the answer. He'd done it to protect her mother's reputation and to inoculate Addie from gossip. But doubts were starting to niggle, and Addie had to decide how far down the rabbit hole she was willing to go to placate Ethan Barrow's obsession.

She hurried along the cobblestone lane, impatient to get back to her vehicle. So deep in thought, she'd lost track of time and her surroundings when she needed to remain focused and vigilant.

Lined with brick walls and lush plantings, the alley lay in deep shade, but a sunlit street glimmered just ahead, like a light at the end of a tunnel. Somewhere behind her, a dog barked. The guttural bay sounded primal and fierce, an animal protecting its turf. Addie registered the commotion but she wasn't concerned. The dog was safely contained within the brick wall, doing what came naturally to a canine guardian. Still, the hair at the back of her neck lifted as the barking dropped to a menacing growl, and for a moment she had visions of gleaming eyes and a predatory prowl.

The barking ceased abruptly. In the eerie quiet, Addie heard the rustle of bushes and the soft thud of what might have been footsteps.

She whirled, hoping to find Ethan trying to catch up with her, but the lane was empty for as far back as she could see. She scanned the shadows, peering into the deepest part of the shade along the wall as her hand went to her bag. She'd heard *something*. The stealthy sound hadn't been her imagination. Had someone disappeared inside a gate?

Farther down the alley, the dog came back to life. The throaty snarls unnerved her as she took a few steps toward the sound.

"Hello? Is someone there?"

She saw him then, a man slipping along the top of the brick wall, crouched and almost hidden from her view by a silvery cascade of Spanish moss. Even after she'd spotted him, she wondered if her eyes were playing tricks on her. His movements were so fluid and furtive, he might have been nothing more than a figment of her imagination. Yet he was right there, hidden in plain sight, and she could have sworn the scent of magnolias emanated from his presence as he drew close.

The perfume overwhelmed her. The whole tableau seemed so dreamlike that she felt disoriented and dazzled from the sunlight shimmering down through a live oak. "I see you on the wall," she called out. "I'm a police detective. Come down with your hands where I can see them."

He remained where he was, shoulders slouched and head bowed so that the hood he'd pulled over his head obscured his features. But Addie knew that he watched her. The power of his gaze was a tangible shiver down her backbone.

She kept a safe distance as she drew her weapon. "I said come down!" When he still didn't comply, she hardened her commands. "Who are you? Why are you following me?"

"Adaline…"

The distorted singsong was identical to the disguised voice she'd heard in the gutted house the night before. He was the same intruder who had left a trail of crimson magnolia petals on her walkway.

She took out her phone to call for backup.

"Adaline…" the altered voice rasped.

"Who are you? What do you want?"

A long pause. Then, "It's time you learn the truth."

She squinted into the light. "What truth?"

"The truth about your mother."

He burst out of the Spanish moss with the shock of a shotgun blast. His speed and agility startled Addie and she stumbled back as he dropped down on the cobblestones in front of her. Her phone clattered to the ground as she clung to her weapon.

He didn't attack even though he momentarily had the advantage. Instead, he turned and dashed back down the alley.

His features had remained hidden, but Addie took note of his size. He wasn't a big man. Average height, average build. She'd faced more physically imposing suspects, but none that had unnerved her more.

She picked up her phone and took off after him. "Police! Stop right there! I said *stop!*"

As abruptly as he'd fled, he halted. His hands came up as he stood with his back to her. Then slowly he turned, head still bowed, but now Addie could see the lower part of his face. Mouth, chin, part of his jawline. His grinning countenance seemed both feral and cunning, and her blood ran cold with dread.

The dog was still barking, louder, closer, a frenetic counterpoint to the man's silent sneer. The sunlight streaming through the oak canopy elongated his shadow, and for a moment, it almost seemed to Addie that something evil crawled along the ground toward her. She inadvertently took a step back as the dog grew more frenzied.

Nails pawed at the wooden gate. The latch and hinges rattled.

Too late, Addie realized she had been lured to this particular spot for a reason. The scent of magnolia seemed to intensify as her fingers tightened on the grip of her weapon.

"Who are you?" she demanded yet again.

His hands were still in the air. Slowly, he unfurled his arms as if he were reaching for the edges of the alley. He opened his hands, and scarlet petals rained down upon the cobblestones. Addie wasn't surprised. She'd known he was her assailant, and yet for one split second, she froze in shock.

His fingertips raked against the brick wall, drawing a deep shudder as Addie tried to intuit his next move. With a flex of his hand, he released the wrought iron latch, and the gate flew open.

Addie saw nothing more than a dark blur with bared teeth and gleaming eyes before she was knocked off her feet. She landed hard on the cobblestones, and the dog was on her in a flash. Instinctively, she lifted her arms to stave off the attack, but a sharp command from behind the wall saved her.

"Thor! Come!"

The German shepherd hovered over her, growling and drooling, and then he turned with a defeated whimper and trotted back through the gate.

The owner came rushing out, effusive with

apologies and explanations as she closed the gate behind her. "Oh, my God, are you okay?"

"Yes, I think so. He didn't bite me. Just knocked me down."

The woman hurried over to offer a hand as Addie scrambled to her feet. "I'm so sorry. Nothing like this has ever happened. He's a good dog, well behaved and obedient. But he's very protective of his turf. If anyone tries to come onto the property, he lets me know." Her tone held a subtle accusation.

"It wasn't his fault." Addie inspected the scrapes on her palms. "I suspect someone provoked him before they let him out."

"Provoked him?" The woman looked outraged. "How?"

"I don't know. Maybe he was goaded through the gate or from over the wall. He may even have been physically incited."

"Why would someone do such a thing?" The woman was clearly upset, so much so that she'd failed to notice Addie's gun. Her eyes widened as Addie slipped the weapon into her bag. She backed away. "What are you doing back here, anyway? Who are you?"

"Detective Adaline Kinsella." Addie presented her shield and ID. "Someone was here a minute ago, a man wearing a hoodie. Average height, average build. You didn't see him when you came through the gate?"

"There was no one back here but you." The woman glanced around uneasily. "Was he the one who tormented my dog? Should I be worried?"

"You've got Thor. You should be fine," Addie said. "Just be on the lookout for any suspicious activity." She handed the woman her card. "Give me a call if you see or hear anything."

The woman hurried back through the gate, leaving Addie alone in the alley. The man in the hood was long gone. Nothing remained of their strange encounter but a trail of crimson magnolia petals.

THE SQUAD CAR had already departed by the time Ethan returned to Naomi Quinlan's house, but he wanted to make certain the black Charger wasn't lurking somewhere nearby. He took a position down the street where he could watch the house without being detected.

After several minutes went by with no sign of countersurveillance, he circled the block and came in through the alley, using Ida's key to let himself in. He went through the house quickly, clearing each room before he returned to the office for a more thorough search. Then he headed down the hallway to the bedroom. He'd just opened a nightstand drawer when a sound checked him. He turned his ear to the hallway, listening for the click of a closing door or the telltale creak of a floorboard. Nothing else came to him, but he had the strongest premonition that he was no longer alone in the house.

Drawing his weapon, he moved silently across the room, flattening himself against the wall as he peered out the door. He listened for a moment longer before slipping down the hallway to inspect the rest of the house. He checked the rear rooms first, easing through the kitchen and onto the sun porch. The windows were closed and the dead bolt on the back door was still engaged. Nothing seemed amiss, and yet Ethan couldn't shake the notion that he had company, well hidden and malevolent.

He opened the door and went down the steps, lingering at the bottom as his gaze moved along the fence line. A mild breeze blew across the garden, rustling the banana trees and stirring a distant wind chime. The sky was clear, the sun warm and bright. Perfect weather to be lying on the beach or drifting on a lake. Not a good day to be searching a dead woman's house.

He went back inside and retraced his steps, examining the windows and doors at the front of the house. Another sound propelled him back into Naomi's office. A black-and-white cat sat atop the desk, cleaning his paws. Ethan's sudden appearance startled him. The cat paused midgrooming, ears back, fur puffed.

Ethan looked around the room and then glanced

over his shoulder into the foyer. Then he moved to the desk. The cat hissed and backed away from him.

"Ferocious, aren't you?" Ethan examined the window locks. "How did you get in here, anyway?" Ida had said something about feeding Naomi's cat, but surely the animal hadn't been locked up in the house since the hit-and-run. He looked healthy enough. Had someone let him in after Ethan and Addie fled earlier?

Ethan went back into the foyer and opened the front door. The cat shot out of the house like a rocket, lunging off the porch and sprinting across the yard to Ida's garden.

Glancing both ways down the street, Ethan closed the door and made his way back down the hallway to Naomi's bedroom. He stood on the threshold, his senses still on alert as he waited for another giveaway sound. When nothing came to him, he set to work, finishing his search of the nightstands and then turning to the dresser. He put away his weapon, but he kept an eye on the door and an ear tuned to the hallway just in case.

After several minutes of intense riffling, he sat back on his heels as he cast his gaze around the room, looking for less obvious hiding places. Then his gaze came back to the dresser. He had a view of the closet in the mirror. The door was ajar. Had it been that way earlier?

He rose silently and moved across the room to throw back the door. Stepping inside, he parted hangers until he was certain the closet was clear. Then his gaze lifted to the ceiling, where a thick cord hung down from the attic door. He released the folding stairs and climbed up, each step creaking and shifting beneath his weight. Another string hung from a light socket attached to a rafter. Ethan clicked on the bulb, but the anemic light chased away only the nearest of shadows.

He hoisted himself up through the opening, hunching his shoulders to avoid the rafters. The area was larger than he would have imagined and partially finished with floors and walls. The space on either side of the furnace accommodated several storage boxes, and someone had created a desk using an old wooden door and two small file cabinets. Colored folders were stacked on top of the desk, and photographs had been thumbtacked to a corkboard wall behind it. For whatever reason, Naomi Quinlan had outfitted a secret office in her attic.

Ethan's impulse was to go straight for those files, but instead he turned to survey the rest of the attic. At the fringes of illumination, he could just make out an old wicker chair and a myriad of plastic lawn ornaments. A one-armed mannequin lay discarded on the floorboards. Someone had tucked a red flower in the nylon strands of her hair and posed her remaining arm across her chest. The staged tableau looked eerily familiar, and a shiver crept up Ethan's spine as he moved in closer.

The mannequin's eyes were glass rather than painted, and the reflection of light gave life to the frozen face. Ethan knelt to touch a finger to the crimson flower petal that had been placed over the molded lips. The dried botanical crumbled at even so light a contact, releasing a musty, funereal scent into the attic.

There was no mistaking the intent. The mannequin had been displayed like a Twilight Killer victim and left for someone to find.

Or was this a private exhibition, a macabre showing for one?

Ethan had only known Naomi Quinlan through her emails, but nothing she had written suggested this kind of ghoulish fascination. He used his phone to snap a few shots before he moved to the other side of the attic. Here, the boxes and forgotten keepsakes had been shoved aside to accommodate a narrow mattress beneath the eaves. Apples and potato chip bags littered the floor around the makeshift bed and a hardback lay open on the pillow. Ethan recognized the title. It was one of the dozens of books that had been written in the aftermath of his father's confinement. He'd read them all in the hope of finding a clue or even flawed logic in the telling of his father's story.

Unlike the dried magnolia petal, the apples appeared fresh. Someone had been here recently.

Using the flashlight app on his phone, Ethan scanned the attic. Satisfied that he hadn't overlooked anything significant—another clue or someone lurking in the shadows—he carried his phone to the desk, angling the beam over the folders before zeroing in on the photographs.

The corkboard had been divided into three sections. The first was comprised of images that had been clipped from newspapers and magazines of Twilight's Children. The second section was all about the killers—newspaper accounts of Orson Lee Finch's arrest and trial, courtroom sketches and even a grainy shot of Ethan's father captured inside the state psychiatric hospital.

The third section contained crime scene and autopsy photographs arranged in chronological order by victim. Ethan was no stranger to gruesome imagery, but the display in Naomi Quinlan's attic took him aback. The photographs could only have come from the official murder files, reinforcing his belief that Naomi or someone close to her had had an important contact in the police department.

Ethan took his time studying the images before turning his attention to the folders. He found more newspaper clippings, manuscript pages and hundreds of handwritten notes and interviews, but no DNA results.

Returning to the corkboard, he scoured the crime-scene photographs with a magnifying glass he found on the desk. The bodies had all been displayed in an identical manner. Arms folded over chest, legs straight, hair fanned about the face.

Ethan's gaze shot to the mannequin. He wanted to believe she was nothing more than a visual inspiration for Naomi's writing, but the mattress shoved up underneath the rafters suggested a darker stimulation.

A sound at the top of the steps caught him off guard, and he whirled as he reached for his weapon. He caught only a glimpse of black-and-white fur before the cat clambered down the stairs and bolted to safety.

Ethan stared down the open hatch into the closet. He heard nothing, saw nothing out of place, but someone had let that cat back in the house.

Possibly the same person who had been living in Naomi Quinlan's attic. An unsub with an unnatural fixation on the Twilight Killer case.

Chapter Nine

Addie walked up and down the alley and then circled the block, looking for the man in the hoodie. She'd never had a good view of his face—probably couldn't pick him out of a lineup—but the disguised voice and the trail of crimson magnolia petals left no doubt that he was the same man who had assaulted her the night before.

What she couldn't figure out was how he'd managed to follow her to and from Naomi Quinlan's house without her or Ethan spotting him. Addie had been careful leaving home that morning, taking a circuitous route out of the neighborhood and then cruising through the downtown streets at a sedate pace while she kept an eye on her rearview mirror.

She was certain she hadn't picked up a tail, and yet someone had managed to track her and Ethan's whereabouts. The police hadn't arrived at Naomi's house out of the blue. Someone had known they were there. If Gwen Holloway was responsible for alerting the cops, had she also sent someone to attack Addie?

Ethan's paranoia was starting to rub off on her, she decided. More likely, her initial assessment had been correct. The man in the alley was one of those fanatical people who did creepy things like write letters to a dead woman's daughter. Only he'd taken the fixation a step further. His behavior had everything to do with Twilight's Children and nothing at all to do with Gwen Holloway. Addie and the other victims' children had always attracted their share of crazies. People were fascinated by serial killers and had been since the term was first coined. That same grisly captivation had propelled profilers like James Merrick to near rock-star status until his downfall had blighted the unit.

Addie paused on the street to glance behind her. She didn't notice anything out of the ordinary. No covert stares or sidelong glances. The pedestrians on the street paid her no attention at all, and yet she couldn't shake the notion that her stalker—as she had now come to think of him— was nearby. That he watched her in amusement from the safety of a shop window or from a shady park bench.

The day was steamy, and yet Addie's blood ran cold. She felt exposed on the street and vulnerable in a way she couldn't explain. It wasn't so much that she feared for her physical safety.

She knew how to handle herself. But she experienced a deeper dread. A festering premonition that old secrets were about to be exposed and her life might never be the same.

A breeze rippled through the leaves, sounding like whispers.

It's time you learn the truth.

The truth about your mother.

A squad car cruised by, and Addie turned her face away, pretending to study a clothing display in a window. Once the car was out of sight, she left the shade of the awning and crossed the intersection at the light. The streets were quickly filling up. Tourists meandered while locals bustled to work or to brunch. Addie kept to the fringes of a sightseeing group, breaking off at the next corner to head back to her vehicle.

She drove straight to police headquarters and entered through the public door, sending her bag and weapon through the metal detector as she presented her ID.

The place was quiet for a weekend morning. She said hello to another detective as she made her way to her desk. He glanced up from his paperwork, bored and eager for a distraction. "Thought you were on vacation, Kinsella."

"I was. Came back early to clear a few things off my desk before Monday morning."

She kept her gaze averted as she sat down at her desk. The last thing she wanted was aimless chitchat. She waited for the detective to return to his work, and then she turned on her computer and entered her password at the prompt. She typed Naomi Quinlan's name in the search bar and glanced around anxiously as she waited for the file to load. The phone on her desk rang, and something—maybe intuition, maybe a movement at the corner of her eye—drew her gaze to the second floor as she picked up the receiver.

She spotted the deputy director gazing down at her as she identified herself to the caller.

He had a cell phone to his ear and nodded when he saw that he had her attention. "Come up," he said into the phone. Then the line went dead.

Addie replaced the receiver, turned off her computer and stood. The detective watched her curiously as she walked past his desk. By the time she'd climbed the stairs, David Cutler had disappeared into his office. He stood at the window, a tall, proud man who had devoted his life to public service. Addie had always thought of him as ageless, but now she noticed a slight stoop to his shoulders and the shimmer of more silver in his hair. Little wonder, she thought. The job eventually took a toll on all of them.

He didn't turn as she hovered in his doorway. He seemed so deep in thought, Addie was reluctant to interrupt him, but finally she said, "You wanted to see me?"

He motioned her in but remained at the window for another moment before he took his place behind his desk. "Have a seat."

Addie told herself she had no reason to feel anxious. She'd done nothing wrong, and she'd known the deputy chief for longer than she could remember. He had been there for her when her mother was murdered, when her grandmother had died of natural causes and all the years in between. He'd been guardian, mentor and champion all rolled into one. That he matched the description of the detective who had gone to see Ida McFall meant nothing. The very idea that he might be responsible for a police cover-up was ludicrous. David Cutler remained the finest man Addie had ever known, and she suddenly felt fiercely protective of him.

He sat back in his chair and rubbed the bridge of his nose. "I'm getting too old for these hours."

"It's the weekend," Addie said. "Why aren't you home cutting the grass or watching a ball game?"

He placed his palm on a stack of paperwork and lifted his hand. "The reports were this high when I came in earlier. Can you imagine what that pile would look like if I waited until Monday?"

"There's always going to be paperwork," Addie said. "You look tired. You should think about taking some time off. Maybe go up to the cabin. The lake is beautiful right now."

He gave her a pained smile. "You've been talking to Helen. Not that either of you has any room to criticize. Her hours are as long as mine, and here you are back from your vacation early. What are you doing here, anyway?"

"I had some loose ends to tie up before Monday. Nothing that can't wait, though, if you'd like to grab lunch."

"Another time," he said with sigh. "I'm glad you came in today. Gives us a chance to talk."

"What's on your mind?"

A frown flicked across his brow as he picked up a pen from his desk, absently weaving it through his fingers. "Did you know Ethan Barrow is in Charleston?"

"He came by the Gainey house yesterday. I was surprised to see him. Actually, *stunned* might be a better word."

"You didn't know he was coming?"

"Not a clue. I hadn't seen or heard from him in ten years."

"No phone calls, no email? No correspondence at all?"

Addie cocked her head. "None of the above. Why the third degree?"

"He came to see me, too." He cast her a glance before returning his attention to the pen. "It was a strange meeting, to say the least."

"Why? What did he say?"

He hesitated. "He wanted to talk about the night your mother died."

Addie sat up in her chair. "What about that night?"

Another frowned flickered as he contemplated her question. "I don't think we need to get into that right now. I thought you should know that he's in town and apparently still laboring under the misconception, or outright delusion, that James Merrick is an innocent man."

Addie tucked back her hair. "You don't think there's a slight possibility he could be right?"

"Don't tell me he's suckered you back in already." He gave her the longest stare, one of those censuring looks that made Addie feel like a guilty teenager. "Let me guess. He's found new evidence."

Addie tried not to fidget under the spotlight of his glare. "He did mention something to that effect."

"Did he also mention the nature of this new evidence?"

She opened her mouth to answer, but something in David Cutler's eyes—a cold, hard gleam—reminded her of Ida McFall's misgivings about the detective who had come to see her. *I think he may have been looking for Naomi's evidence. I'm certain he was fishing for something.*

What if the man Ida had spoken to was no longer a detective, but the deputy chief? Her description matched. It might also explain why he hadn't given her a name. But why would the deputy chief take an interest in Naomi Quinlan's hit-and-run?

Addie didn't like the direction of her thoughts. She didn't like the worrisome doubts that were starting to burrow beneath her affection for David Cutler and undermine her faith in him.

"You should probably talk to him about it," Addie said.

"I'm asking you."

She shrugged. "All I know is that a local woman contacted him. Apparently, she was writing a book about the Twilight Killer case and had turned up something in the course of her research. Before he could come to Charleston to meet with her in person, she was killed in a hit-and-run. Could be just a coincidence. Or maybe she really was onto something. We may never know. Anyway, her name was Naomi Quinlan. I caught the call the night she died, but by the time I arrived on the scene, Detective Yates had assumed control. Since I was in the middle of a transfer, I didn't raise a stink about turf. But the timing of her death is curious, to say the least."

"I hope you're not implying that Detective Yates or anyone else in this department had something to do with that woman's death."

His conclusion surprised Addie. "I'm not saying anything of the sort. I meant just what I said. Naomi Quinlan contacted Ethan about her research, and then she turned up dead before he could meet with her in person. The timing *is* curious."

"Does any of this really surprise you, Addie? Ethan Barrow has a nose for trouble."

"I know that. But he only arrived in town two days ago. He can hardly be blamed for Naomi Quinlan's hit-and-run. And even though I may not agree with his methods, I can't fault him for wanting to clear his father's name."

"You're still defending him."

His accusatory tone rankled. Addie waited a beat before she responded. "Seeing his side of things doesn't equate with defending him. A child, no matter the age, needs to believe the best about a parent. I'm no different. I know my mother wasn't perfect, but I still like to think that she loved me more than anything. That I was the most important person in her life."

"She did. You were."

Addie smiled. "I may remember more about my mother than you think."

His expression darkened. "What's that supposed to mean?"

"Nothing." She paused with another shrug. "Funny thing about those memories. Most days I can barely recall what she looked like, and then I'll smell a flower or hear a song and it's like she's right there with me. Helen and I were talking about this just yesterday. Out of the blue, I remembered a whole conversation from the night my mother died."

His demeanor never changed, but Addie sensed a sudden tension. "What conversation?"

"I overheard you and Helen talking in the hallway outside my bedroom. She was very upset. She wondered how she would tell me what happened. You told her to let me sleep, that the news could wait until morning."

"You talked to Helen about this?"

Addie nodded. "I'm afraid I upset her. She always looks so sad when my mother's name is brought up."

"She was very fond of Sandra. We both were. I don't think either of us has ever really gotten over the loss. She was such a vibrant person. A big believer in living life to the fullest. I still think of her as a bright star gone dark too soon."

"That's a lovely sentiment." Addie studied his expression. Despite his gracious words about her mother, he suddenly seemed pensive and unsettled.

"It's true," he said with a sigh. "Sandy could walk through a door and light up a room."

Sandy. Something in his voice shifted when he said her mother's name. Addie hadn't heard anyone refer to Sandra Kinsella by her nickname in a very long time. "Tell me about the night she died."

He flicked her a troubled glance. "So you can convey whatever I say to Ethan Barrow?"

His rebuke stung, although Addie supposed she deserved it. She'd thought—hoped—they'd long ago moved past her betrayal. "I would never do that, but you only have my word. If I haven't proved my loyalty and dedication to you by now, I guess I never will."

"I'm sorry," he said. "That was a cheap shot."

She nodded her acceptance. "I understand why you have reservations about Ethan Barrow, but this isn't about him. What happened to my mother changed my life. Her murder changed us all. You said yourself you and Helen have never gotten over it. Hearing about that night might help me understand some of my unresolved issues."

He stared down at his desk, looking as if he would rather be anywhere at that moment than in his office with Addie. She understood what she was asking. Digging up the past pained her, too, but too much had been swept under the rug for the sake of sparing her feelings. She needed to hear a firsthand account of that night.

He glanced up with a deep scowl. "This won't be easy to hear."

"I know."

"You're sure you want this?"

"Yes."

His gaze dropped back to the desk. "I worked late that night. Not unusual back in those days. These days, either, for that matter. My partner and I had gone out for a beer and a bite to eat after our watch. He went home to his family, but I came back here to have another look at a case file. You always think you've missed something. Just one more glance at the crime-scene photos or another reading of the eyewitness statements and you'll find that elusive piece of the puzzle."

Addie nodded, though he barely seemed aware of her presence now. She studied him furtively, wondering what had caused the deep furrows in his brow and the new creases around his mouth and eyes.

"Helen called around two in the morning. I'd fallen asleep at my desk, and the phone woke me up. She was very upset. Almost hysterical. She said that Sandra had promised to pick you up before ten. You had a doctor's appointment first thing the next morning, and she didn't want to have to come by our place to get you. When she didn't show, Helen was certain something had happened. I reminded her that your mother wasn't always the most reliable, that she was probably out with friends and time got away from her, but Helen wouldn't be calmed."

"Why did she wait so long to call you?"

"We were both burning the candle at both ends. Helen had just started her practice, and she was under a lot of stress. She'd fallen asleep on the couch watching the news. When she woke up and realized she hadn't heard from Sandra, she became frantic."

"And I slept through it all," Addie murmured.

"She had no reason to wake you. We were still hoping for the best. Helen stayed with you while I went out looking for Sandra. I can still remember how quiet the streets seemed that night. Almost ghostly. The clouds had moved out, and the moon was up. It cast the strangest glow over the city. Not soft and misty as one tends to think of moonlight, but cold and harsh and so brilliant it seemed as if you could peer into the darkest corners and find evil staring back at you."

Addie shivered at his description, at the distant look in his eyes and the tinge of dread in his voice. She could almost imagine herself in the car with him, riding shotgun as they searched for her murdered mother.

"You and Sandy lived in a little house just north of Calhoun. Your grandmother had bought the place after you were born so that you could have a proper home. That same house on that same street would cost a small fortune these days, but back then, people like us could still afford to buy downtown. Helen and I lived only a few blocks over."

"I remember that house," Addie said. "I still drive by now and then."

"It was dark when I arrived. I got out of the car and knocked on the door. When no one answered, I circled around to the back and searched the yard. I kept telling myself there was no reason to worry. Sandy always lost track of time. She was out having fun and would apologize profusely in the morning when she came to pick you up. But deep down I knew something was wrong. I could feel it in my gut. You work cases for as long as I have, you develop a sixth sense."

Even though Addie knew how the story ended, she found herself pressing forward, gripping the armrests of her chair as she shivered. "What did you do?"

"I got back in the car and drove through the neighborhood looking for her. I found her two blocks over. She was in a narrow alley that ran between two streets. You may remember it. Your mother always loved taking those shortcuts. She said those alleys were Charleston's secret passageways. Not everyone knew about them."

"We used to go out on Sunday afternoons looking for them," Addie said.

He gave a vague nod. "If I hadn't already been on alert, I might not have seen her. She was just a shadow within a deeper shadow. When I moved in closer, though, I saw the blood. The puddle had already started to congeal. She had been there for a while." He seemed to catch himself then and glanced up to gauge her reaction.

"Go on," Addie said. "I want to hear the rest."

"It's not something a daughter needs to hear about her mother."

"Tell me anyway."

"She was posed. Arms folded over her chest,

hair fanned out around her face, clothing arranged just so. That kind of attention to detail takes time, and yet no one had come out to investigate or called the police. No one saw or heard anything. I still ask myself how that could be. Not a single witness saw her die. Not a single person heard her scream."

"It was late. You said yourself the streets were empty."

"Yes. When I realized *how* she was posed, my first thought was that we'd made a terrible mistake. We'd arrested the wrong man. Orson Lee Finch was in jail awaiting trial, but how could he be guilty of all those other murders when the Twilight Killer had struck again? Then I noticed subtle differences in the way the body had been laid out. Sandy's left arm was folded over her right instead of the other way around. The hair was different, too, and the clothing. Discrepancies so slight only someone who had spent hours scrutinizing crime-scene photos from Finch's spree would have picked up on them. It was like the killer wanted me to find them. Like those clues had been left just for me."

"Gwen Holloway noticed the clues, too, didn't she? You helped her write the profile."

That roused him from the spell, and his frown deepened. "I gave her my input, sure. But that night, even after I noticed the inconsistencies, I couldn't process what it all meant. In the back of my mind, I was already thinking copycat, but I couldn't formulate a coherent theory. I was still in shock when the first patrol car arrived. Then the detectives came, forensics, the coroner. At some point, I drove home. Helen waited at the window. She met me at the door. I didn't have to say a word because she already knew."

"You've never told me any of this," Addie said.

"I couldn't bring myself to tell you, even after you became a cop. I didn't want those terrible images to sully your mother's memory. I wanted you to remember Sandy as she was. Maybe I wanted to remember her that way, too. A free spirit, infuriatingly irresponsible at times, but beautiful inside and out. She loved you, Addie."

"I loved her, too. She was a complicated woman. Secretive and oftentimes selfish. I'm not sure I ever really knew her, but I did love her. I understand why you've always tried to protect me, but sometimes the truth is the only thing that can heal old wounds."

A bitter edge crept into his voice. "And sometimes the truth just rips them wide-open again."

"So you had her case files sealed," Addie said. "You knew as soon as I joined the department that I would go looking for them."

"The case files have always been available to you," he said.

"Not all of them."

"You didn't need to see the photographs."

"Or the autopsy report?" She clasped her hands in her lap. "I know why you did what you did."

His gaze shot to her. He seemed on the verge of a denial and then thought better of it. "What are you talking about?"

"You didn't want me to find out that my mother was pregnant."

His eyes closed briefly. "What purpose would that knowledge have served? It only made the tragedy that much harder to accept."

"But I already knew. The autopsy report was merely confirmation."

His head came up. "Before you accessed the files? How?"

"She told me."

Her simple statement seemed to stun him anew. "But you were just a child. She shouldn't have put that burden on you. Why did you never say anything?"

Now it was Addie who grew pensive and hesitant. Twenty-five years after her mother's murder, and she still felt as if she were betraying a confidence. "She told me not to tell anyone, even my grandmother. She said it had to be our secret. People would be hurt when they found out, and she needed to decide how best to deal with the fallout."

He rubbed a hand across his eyes. "I wish you would have come to me."

"There were times when I wanted to, but my

mother's secret was the last thing I had of her. It bonded us. And whether I realized it or not, I needed to protect her."

His gaze softened. "You understand, then, why I wanted to do the same."

She nodded. "I do. You were worried what people would say about her and how that gossip would affect me. But she died twenty-five years ago. Hardly the Dark Ages. No one would have cared about her pregnancy."

"Don't kid yourself, Addie. The more things change, the more they stay the same. People will always judge."

She wanted to argue his point, but deep down, she knew he was right. "Is that why you're worried about Ethan Barrow? Are you afraid he'll rip open all those old wounds?"

"I worry about your wounds, Addie."

"I can take care of myself."

"Under other circumstances, I would agree, but that man caused a lot of damage ten years ago. Not just to this department but to you personally. He coerced you into accessing those sealed files, and to what end? So that he could cherry-pick information to feed to the press in order to taint the investigation. He tried to free his father by jeopardizing this department's reputation and Finch's conviction. He was devious and manipulative, and I don't see that he's changed much in that regard. But you have, Addie. You've grown into a damn fine investigator. You earned your detective shield and the respect of your peers the hard way. Everyone in this department recognizes your talent and dedication. You may be interested to know that your selection to Gwen Holloway's program came as a unanimous decision." He sat back in his chair and folded his arms. "You've worked too hard to throw it all away on another bad decision. Think before you act."

"I will. I always do."

"I hope so," he said, but his tone sounded doubtful.

He picked up his pen and opened a folder in dismissal. Addie got up and walked to the door, turning to study his bowed head before she went back downstairs to continue her work. The conversation left her sad and unsettled. It wasn't so much his account of her mother's murder scene that upset her. Addie had known the basic facts for years. It was the look in his eyes, the odd note in his voice. She tried to shake off her uneasiness, but she'd never seen David Cutler look so worn-out, and she wondered if Helen had been right to worry about his health.

Or was it something other than the job that had hollowed his cheeks and shadowed his eyes?

Addie looked up to find him watching her from the second-story railing. Their gazes clung for a moment before she turned back to her computer with a shiver.

Chapter Ten

Ethan waited on the porch steps when Addie got home late that afternoon. She pulled into the driveway and parked, taking her time to gather her things before exiting the vehicle.

Her conversation with David Cutler still lingered, and his warning had not fallen on deaf ears. Ethan Barrow was trouble, but Addie couldn't put all the blame on his shoulders. She had free will. She was the one who had allowed herself to be drawn back into an ill-advised investigation, but it wasn't too late to right things. All she had to do was get out of the car and send Ethan packing. Come Monday morning, she could start her training with a clear head and enjoy this new phase of her career. She could seize the opportunity and run with it. Get on with her life as if the past two days had been nothing more than a glitch.

But that wasn't going to happen, and Addie knew it. From the moment she'd agreed to hear Ethan out, her course had been charted, and now things were moving too quickly to turn back.

Someone had assaulted her, stalked her and loosed a dog on her. She wasn't convinced those incidents were connected to Ethan's investigation or to Naomi Quinlan's DNA evidence, but at the very least, questions had been raised. Doubts were stirring. What if her mother's killer was still out there somewhere? What if the murderer was someone close to her, someone she knew, respected, someone she would least expect? If she walked away now, would she be able to live with those uncertainties?

Addie had been so young when her mother died and so devastated by the loss that she'd never thought to question the official investigation. As she grew older, certain things had crossed her mind—the paternity of her mother's baby, for one thing. Even now, she had no idea who the father was. She barely knew her own dad. Her mother had kept her social life completely separate from their home life. All Addie had ever been told about the pregnancy was to say nothing.

It has to be our little secret for now, Addie. Do you understand what that means?

I can't tell anyone.

No one. Not even Grandma. People would be upset if they knew.

Why?

It's grown-up stuff. You don't need to worry about it.

Mama?

Yes, Addie?

Will the baby live with us?

Would you like that?

I wouldn't mind. She could stay in my room and I could take care of her like Aunt Helen takes care of me.

Is that what you think? That Helen is the one who takes care of you?

Don't be mad, Mama. What did I do?

You didn't do anything, sweet girl. And I'm not mad. I just wish... Never mind what I wish. Actions speak louder than words. Things are going to change around here, Addie. That's a promise. From now on, I'm going to be the best mother I can be to you.

And to the baby?

We'll see.

Addie hadn't thought about that conversation in years. She hadn't let herself dwell on the consequences of her mother's pregnancy, hadn't dared to acknowledge the suspicions that had glimmered at the edge of her subconscious since childhood. Those doubts threatened her peace of mind now, but she ruthlessly cut them out before they could take root. But as her mother's voice flitted away, another, more sinister one took its place.

It's time you learn the truth.

The truth about your mother.

She glanced across the yard at Ethan. He stared back at her. The power of his gaze penetrated the car window, and Addie shivered. His father had killed her mother. As much as Ethan want to clear James Merrick's name, Addie needed to believe in his guilt. Because the alternative was unfathomable.

She got out of the car and started across the grass toward him. He rose to greet her. "What's wrong?"

"Who said anything's wrong?" Her retort sounded sharper than she meant it. She took a breath and tried to relax, but his insight grated. She didn't like that he could read her so easily.

His gaze turned mildly reproachful. "I know you, Addie. I can tell when something is bothering you."

"No, you used to know me, but that was a long time ago."

"Or maybe I still know you better than you'd like to admit."

She sighed. "It's been a long day. Let's just leave it at that." She sat down on the porch. "I won't ask how you found out where I live, but I am curious how you got here. I don't see a vehicle anywhere."

"I took a cab to the neighborhood entrance and then walked the rest of the way." He sat down beside her. "I thought it was safer that way."

"You're still that certain Gwen Holloway is having you followed?"

"I'm that certain someone has eyes on me, yes.

The cops showing up at Naomi Quinlan's house proved that."

"Ida could have called them."

"Why would she do that?"

Addie turned to give him a measuring look. "I don't know, Ethan. I don't know about a lot of things lately. You don't just bring trouble. You bring confusion. Chaos. You're exhausting. I feel worn-out already."

"Is that your way of asking me to leave?"

"No, sit down. It's my way of venting."

He sat back down. "I understand your frustration, but we're getting close. We're rattling cages, and someone is getting nervous."

"It says a lot that you think that's a good thing."

"How else will we find the truth?"

She could sense a nervous tension in him, an excitement that bubbled and brewed just below the surface. His anticipation was almost a tangible thing and more than a little infectious. Addie's heart thudded as she studied his profile. She couldn't help but admire the curl of his lashes, the straight line of his nose, the curvature of his lips. He was a very attractive man, more so now than a decade ago, because all those years on the job had seasoned and hardened him while all his secrets and obsessions kept him vulnerable. Addie found herself irrevocably drawn to him, even though he had once been her downfall and could be again if she wasn't careful. She supposed that said a lot about her.

He turned to her then, his expression inscrutable. If he had an inkling of her thoughts, his demeanor didn't betray him. "I found something at Naomi Quinlan's house that you should know about."

She drew a quick breath. "The DNA results?"

"No, not that, unfortunately. But I did stumble across an interesting cache in the attic. I found notes and manuscript pages from her book project and some of the police reports and crime-scene photos from the Twilight Killer case files. Given Naomi's age and her aunt's connection to the case, I think we can safely assume that Vivian DuPriest is the one who had the police contact. We should go talk to her. She may know about the DNA results. It's possible she acquired a portion of the original sample twenty-five years ago."

"I agree we should talk to her, but the leaker may not have been a cop," Addie said. "Vivian probably had sources in the coroner's office as well as the lab."

"I'm sure she did, but regardless of the original source, the material ended up in Naomi's possession. She's the one who ran the sample through the databases. From what I saw in the attic, her research was well organized. The photos and newspaper clippings were arranged in three distinct categories—Twilight's Children, the killers and the victims."

Addie was horrified. "She had pictures of me in her attic?"

"She had images of all the children. You should see that place. It was like she—or someone—had set up a hidden office. I saw a mattress up there, too. The area was littered with fruit and soft drink cans. Someone has been staying up there since her death."

"This just gets better and better," Addie said with a shiver. The scenario sounded straight out of a scary movie. Someone taking up residence in a dead woman's attic.

Dark scenes bombarded Addie, but she tried to corral her imagination. "What makes you think Naomi didn't set up the bed? If she thought her DNA discovery had put her in danger, she may have felt the need for a hiding place in case someone came looking for the results."

"Anything's possible, but some of the apples looked fresh. I noticed other odd things, too. A cat got inside the house twice after I locked the doors. And an old mannequin had been placed on the floor and posed like one of Finch's victims."

That stopped Addie cold. She stared at him for another long moment as she hugged her arms around her middle. "Posed...how?"

"She was missing an arm, but the other one was crossed over her chest. Her hair was fanned out around her head, and a dried flower petal had been placed over her lips."

"A crimson magnolia petal." It wasn't a question.

He nodded. "I had the crime-scene photos right in front of me. There was no mistaking the pose."

"This is starting to freak me out a little," Addie admitted. "We're not the only ones rattling cages."

"Apparently not."

"What's this about a cat getting inside the house?"

"Yeah, that was strange." Ethan's hand rested on the step between them. Addie had the strongest urge to link her fingers through his and hold on tight, because this was getting to be a very bumpy—not to mention, creepy—ride. "I first saw the cat in Naomi's office. When I opened the front door, it ran outside, and then a little while later, I saw the same cat at the top of the attic steps."

"How do you know it was the same cat?"

"It was black and white just like the one in the office. If you think back, Ida McFall said Naomi gave her a house key so that she could feed the cat. As in a singular feline. Either the cat has a secret way in and out of the house, or someone let it back in."

"Someone with a key."

"Exactly."

"Which means that person was in the house with you."

"It's possible."

Addie glanced around the neighborhood and then stood abruptly. The streets were still sunlit, the lawns green and dotted with color. But a pall had been cast, and now Addie found herself peering around corners in search of sinister silhouettes. "Let's go inside. I could use a drink."

Ethan followed her up the steps and into the tiny foyer. She punched in the security code and then turned to survey the entrance with a frown.

"What is it?" he asked.

She opened the door and examined the lock. "I don't know. I just had the strangest sensation. Maybe it's all our talk about keys and someone being in the house, but…" She glanced over her shoulder as she closed the door. "Have you ever had the feeling when you go home at night that someone has been in your house? It's nothing concrete. Nothing has gone missing. Everything is in its proper place, but the air just feels different."

He walked over and glanced out the window before turning to scan the living area. "You think someone was here while you were out? Who else knows your security code?"

"Helen and David Cutler. Matt Lepear. A cleaning service I use occasionally. I can't think of anyone else other than the security company where I purchased the system."

"Why does your partner know your security code?"

She gave him an exasperated glance. "That's your takeaway?" She shook her head. "He crashed here for a while after his second wife kicked him out. I never got around to changing the code. Not that I need to. I've trusted him with my life for the past ten years." The comment hung like an uneasy accusation between them. Addie had never consciously compared the two men. Matt was her partner. Of course she trusted him. Ethan continued to be both a frustration and a mistake, but there was no denying their chemistry. There seemed to be no dousing that spark.

Ethan watched her curiously. "Is there any reason one of the Cutlers would come by while you were out?"

"I was with the deputy chief earlier after I left you. Helen came over yesterday to feed the stray cats that hang around the backyard, but I can't think of any reason she would have been here today. She knows I'm home from vacation." They walked through the living area and into the kitchen. Addie opened the refrigerator and took out two icy bottles of beer. "You know what else is odd? I woke up last night with the same feeling. I was certain someone had been in the house. I even got up to look around. It turned out to be nothing. The alarm was set, the doors all locked. I was probably still wound up from finding those flower petals on my walkway. Not to mention being cold-cocked." She touched the bandage at her temple. "My anxiety spilled over into my sleep."

"Anyone would be on edge after all that." He took the opener from her hand and uncapped the bottles.

"And I haven't even told you everything." Addie went around and perched on a bar stool. "The guy who hit me? I saw him again today."

Ethan sat down beside her. "Where? When?"

"After I left the churchyard this morning. I took a shortcut through an alley like you suggested, and he came up behind me."

"Why didn't you call me?"

"It happened so fast, I didn't even have time to call for backup. But there's no doubt in my mind he was the guy. Same height, same build. And he used a voice disguiser like he did last night. You can get those everywhere these days for less than twenty bucks. He probably clipped the microphone inside his hoodie so that I couldn't see it."

"Could you tell what he looked like?"

"No, he kept that hood pulled around his face so that I never got a good look at him."

Ethan frowned. "You said he used a voice disguiser. What did he say?"

Addie hesitated. "The whole encounter was pretty unnerving. When I said he came up behind me, he was actually on top of a brick wall, almost hidden by foliage. I'm not sure I would have seen him at all except for a dog behind the wall that kept going crazy. I knew something was wrong. Even after I spotted him up there, I thought I might be imagining things. It was just so bizarre to see him creeping along that wall, and I've seen a lot of weird things in this city. He called out my name. *Adaline. Adaline.* Just like that." She ran a hand up and down her chilled arm. "So creepy."

"That's all he said? Just your name?"

"He said it was time I learn the truth about my mother." She kept rubbing at the goose bumps as if she could scrub away the memory of his taunt.

Ethan lifted his beer and then set it back down. "What do you think he meant by that?"

"Who knows? He jumped off the wall, startled me, and then he fled. I gave chase, but…he got away."

Ethan searched her face. "Why do I have a feeling there's more to the story than you're telling me?"

"I've given you the highlights. Anyway, what I'd like to know is how he found me in the first place. He must have followed us to Naomi's house and then he tailed me from the churchyard. Maybe he's the one who called the cops." She paused in alarm. "You don't think he's the one who's been staying in the attic, do you?"

"He's a person of interest, to say the least."

Addie let out a breath. "I've tried to write him off as just another weirdo who's latched onto one of Twilight's Children—me—but I can't forget what you said about that mannequin and how she was posed with a magnolia petal on her lips. What if whoever is staying in Naomi's attic isn't just someone fascinated with the Twilight Killer case? What if he's practicing to *be* the Twilight Killer?"

"It's a leap, but the thought has crossed my mind."

That Ethan didn't immediately dismiss her theory worried Addie even more.

The house suddenly seemed unnaturally quiet. Even the hum of the refrigerator sounded menacing. Was her stalker out there right now watching her place? Was he imagining her prone and posed, gushing blood from a fatal stab wound to her heart as he placed a magnolia petal upon her frozen lips?

Addie shook herself and glanced at Ethan. "Maybe we're both letting our imaginations get the better of us."

"Maybe we are. We need to remain objective. We don't know enough to draw any conclusions at this point, but the hoodie guy bears finding and watching."

"Right now, he's the one who keeps finding me," Addie said. "I'm certain I wasn't tailed when I left the neighborhood this morning, and we were both careful when we walked to Naomi's house.

So how did he know we would be there? How did he know I would be in the alley at that precise time?"

"If he's the one staying in the attic, he could have followed us out of the house when the police showed up. Did you have your phone with you this morning?"

"Yes, of course. I always do."

"That's another possible explanation. GPS has opened doors for law enforcement and criminals alike. It doesn't take much sophistication for either to track a cell phone. All anyone would need is your number, and not even that with the right equipment and know-how. You should probably use a burner until we resolve this."

"You know I can't do that. I'm a cop. I can't go off the grid because some sicko has decided to play mind games with me."

"Gwen Holloway's program starts on Monday, right? Your whereabouts won't be a secret, anyway. Use a burner when you're off the clock and when you're working on our investigation."

Our investigation. Addie inwardly winced.

"What else did you have in your bag this morning besides your phone and your gun?"

She thought for a moment. "My shield and ID. My car key. A tube of lip gloss."

"Have you had your car worked on lately? Used a car wash or a valet service? A tracker or transmitter can be powered using the battery in a key fob. If you've got a spare, switch it out. Change the code on your security system, too. Do it now before you forget. Then get the locks on your doors changed as soon as possible."

"Changing the locks is no small expense," she said. "Maybe we're overreacting."

"Come on, Addie. You know better than to take chances."

"Okay. I'll call a locksmith in the morning."

Ethan sat drinking his beer while she returned to the foyer to reprogram the security panel. She came back with cell phone in hand. "I don't care if this guy is tracking my number. I'm starving and I'm using this phone to order a pizza. Any objections or requests?"

"No objections. Your vehicle is parked in the driveway. Anyone watching the house would already know you're home."

"Requests?"

"Are you inviting me to dinner?"

Something in his voice, a quiet intimacy, quickened Addie's pulse, but she tried to downplay her reaction with a shrug. "We both have to eat. No anchovies or olives, correct?"

"You remembered."

"Don't be flattered. No anchovies is a given, and I don't like olives, either."

"I remember."

She started to retort, needed to retort so that her defenses remained fortified. Instead, she went into the kitchen to call the neighborhood pizzeria, keeping her back to Ethan while she gathered her poise. When she turned, he was at the kitchen door staring out into the backyard.

"Mind if I have a look around?" he asked.

"Knock yourself out."

Addie didn't follow him. She needed another beat to collect her thoughts. She tried to tell herself she was tired and on edge, but spending so much time with Ethan had made her feel things she hadn't experienced in a very long time. The flutter of her heart at his nearness. Her keen awareness of his heated gaze. She'd forgotten what it was like—the thrill and the terror—to be in those first throes of sexual attraction.

Addie had dated enough after their breakup to know the kind of connection she'd felt with Ethan was rare. He wasn't like any man she'd ever known. He was intense and introspective, someone she knew she should run from. But Addie had discovered that with all those dark emotions came deep passion, the kind that had made her lose coherent thought and good sense. She'd known using David Cutler's computer to open sealed files was morally wrong and professionally indefensible, but she hadn't cared. Not in that moment. One touch, one kiss, one whisper in her ear and she would have done anything for Ethan Barrow.

She was older now, wiser, harder and a lot more jaded. Because of Ethan, she didn't trust easily, and she'd vowed to never again be taken in by a pair of dark eyes and knowing hands. And yet when she watched him now as he moved about her backyard, all she could think about were those eyes staring down at her in a dim room, his hands sliding slowly up her thighs, parting her, teasing her until the only thing she cared about was having him inside her.

She picked up her beer, gulped it down and then, squaring her shoulders, she opened the door and went outside to join him.

He was hunkered on the walkway staring up at the broken security light. He glanced her way when he heard the door. "When did this happen?"

"Last night."

"Before or after you tangled with the suspect?"

"After. Actually, it happened while Matt was still here. We heard a crash and came out to investigate. I think someone threw a rock and took it out."

"Someone?"

"Most likely the same suspect." Addie sat down on the porch steps. The sun was just sinking below the treetops, but the air was still hot. She peeled her ponytail off the back of her neck as she tracked Ethan's movements. He'd changed his clothes since last she'd seen him. By comparison, she felt grungy, cranky and in bad need of a shower. The day seemed never ending. All the angst over the stalker and her unfinished business with Ethan…the conversation with David Cutler that still niggled at the back of her mind. It all took a toll.

She got up and brushed her hands on the sides of her jeans. "I'm going in to take a shower," she said. "I'll leave money on the bar for the pizza. Can you listen for the doorbell?"

"Yes, don't worry. I'll take care of it."

Addie went back inside and headed down the hallway to the bathroom. She started the shower, and while the water heated, she went into the bedroom to lay out clean clothes. Tossing fresh underwear on the bed, she opened the top drawer of her chest and removed her picture box.

After her grandmother died, Addie had become the keeper of the family photographs. She opened the lid and riffled through the cherished images until she found the picture that she wanted. It was a shot of her mother with David and Helen Cutler.

Addie had always loved the photograph, but now as she stared down at their smiling faces, the unlikeliness of their friendship struck her. Their disparate personalities were reflected in the way they each presented themselves. Addie's mother wore a halter top, shorts and her signature red lipstick, her overt sexiness a stark contract to Helen's earth-mother persona and David's stoicism. Sandra stood in the middle—always the center of attention—with her arm linked through Helen's, but she stared up at David. He looked straight into the camera, not smiling, not scowling, but something about his posture, an almost infinitesimal lean toward Addie's mother, reminded her of the way he'd said her mother's nickname. *Sandy.* A bright star gone dark too soon.

Had her mother known she was pregnant when that photo was taken? Had David Cutler?

Addie put the picture box away, but she propped the photograph against her mirror so that she could study it later. So that she could dissect her mother's catlike smile and that dark glint in David Cutler's eyes.

And the faint worry lines etched in Helen Cutler's brow.

Chapter Eleven

A few hours later, Ethan stood at Addie's front window staring out at the dark street. They'd spent a pleasant evening over beer and pizza, and when it had come time for him to head back to his hotel, she'd stunned him by suggesting that he spend the night.

"It's late and I have a spare bedroom, extra toothbrush, everything you need. What's the point in calling a cab at this hour?"

"Are you sure?"

"It's no big deal. The most that will happen is that we'll both get a good night's sleep and then tomorrow morning, we can go see Vivienne Du-Priest together."

But it was a very big deal to Ethan. Addie could have sent him away the moment she saw him on her front steps. He was certain that had been her first inclination. Instead, she'd invited him in for drinks, dinner and a sleepover. If that didn't constitute a major step forward in their relationship, he didn't know what would.

Still, he knew better than to get ahead of himself or to read too much into a gesture too soon. The worst thing he could possibly do was push Addie in a direction she didn't want to go, and Ethan was more than a little gun-shy himself. What if instead of proving his father's innocence he only cemented his guilt? How would Addie feel about him then? How would he feel about himself?

For years, Ethan had lived in the shadow of James Merrick's dark deed. For years, he'd tried to tell himself the sins of his father had no power over him. Unlike James, Ethan had grown up in a stable home with a mother he loved and a stepfather he respected. He'd had all the advantages, gone to all the right schools, had companionship whenever he craved it. He was a loner by choice, not necessity. He was dedicated and persistent, not obsessive. He wasn't his father's son.

But there was no fooling DNA. Ethan supposed it was ironic that in a very real sense, his future now hinged on someone else's DNA.

There was no fooling chemistry, either. The more time he spent in Addie's company, the deeper his attraction. Whether she wanted to admit it or not, she felt something for him, too. He saw a glimmer in her eyes now and then, heard a certain timbre in her voice on those rare occasions when she let down her guard. But Ethan wouldn't let himself revel in her lapses, and he certainly had no intention of taking advantage of her confusion. If anything, he wanted to protect her.

Leaving the window, he made the rounds through the house. Addie had turned in some time ago. Her door was closed, and Ethan stood for a moment listening to the quiet before he went into the bathroom to brush his teeth and wash up.

In the guest room, he peeled off his clothes and climbed under the covers in his boxers. The bed was comfortable and the temperature pleasant, but he couldn't fall asleep for a long time. He watched the rotation of the ceiling fan until he finally grew drowsy.

The shrill blast of the security alarm woke him some time later.

He bolted upright while simultaneously reaching for his weapon. Rising, he moved silently across the floor and stepped into the hallway just as Addie came out of her room. She wore a T-shirt that hit her midthigh, and her hair flowed loosely about her shoulders and down her back. She took aim when she first saw him and then instantly refocused. They went down the hallway together. The front door stood open.

Clearing the immediate area, Ethan went out on the porch. Addie came up behind him after she'd turned off the alarm. "What's going on? Do you see anything?"

"There!" He pointed to a darting silhouette a few houses down. "He's cutting through your neighbor's backyard. Get in the car and see if you can head him off at the next street."

Ethan was down the steps and on the sidewalk before he remembered that he was barefoot and in his underwear. Propriety didn't stop him, nor did the bite of cracked concrete as he pounded after his quarry. He sprinted for the bushes, lifting himself easily over the fence and then pausing to listen for footfalls. He heard Addie's car start up behind him. The engine faded as she made the block.

He moved through the yard, weapon ready, senses alert. A dog barked nearby, and as he turned toward the sound, he glimpsed the interloper from the corner of his eye. The man wore a dark hoodie that blended almost seamlessly with the shadows. Ethan whirled, but before he could close in, the suspect disappeared. Just…vanished.

Ethan wondered if his eyes were playing tricks on him, but as he cautiously approached the back of the fence, he realized an opening had been created in the slats through which the man had slipped.

Easing through, Ethan hugged the side of the house as he made his way out to the sidewalk. The suspect was nowhere to be seen.

A vehicle came toward him without lights. Ethan recognized the car. He stepped off the curb into the street, forcing the Charger to stop. Then he rapped on the glass until the driver lowered the window.

Ethan ducked his head so that he could see both agents. The driver stared up at him while the passenger kept his head turned toward the side window. "Let me guess. You just happened to be in the neighborhood."

The driver shrugged. "Why not? Last time I checked, it's still a free country."

"I would think the FBI could find a better use of your time," Ethan said. "You're not denying you're federal agents, are you?"

"Not denying or confirming anything. Just minding our business."

"Minding your own business, huh?" Ethan glanced at the passenger. His face remained suspiciously averted. "I'd like to see some ID."

"Show us yours first." The driver looked to be in his mid-to late thirties, with dark hair and a cocky attitude.

"You know who I am," Ethan said. "And we all know why you're here. Is this a sanctioned surveillance?"

"I don't know what you're talking about."

"Someone broke into Detective Kinsella's house just now. I don't suppose you know anything about that, either."

"We don't break into houses, Special Agent Barrow. That's more your thing."

"So you do know who I am."

"Let's just say your reputation precedes you."

"Oh, I'm sure Gwen Holloway has briefed you well." Ethan glanced at the second agent, trying to get a sense of his age and body type. "The suspect was on foot and wearing a dark hoodie. Average height, average build. You're certain you didn't catch a glimpse of him?"

"We didn't see anything." The driver paused. "But let's say, hypothetically speaking, that we *were* watching Detective Kinsella's house tonight. You know how surveillance works. We would have maintained a discreet distance. Anyone approaching or fleeing her house on foot would have gone undetected if he knew what he was doing."

"Mind turning on your dome light?" Ethan asked.

"What for?" the agent asked in surprise.

"Your partner has kept his face hidden this whole time. Makes me wonder."

"Nothing to wonder about. He's just shy."

"Is that why you refuse to show me your credentials?" Ethan pressed. "Not that I'll have a hard time figuring out who you are."

"You go right ahead and try, Agent Barrow."

Ethan's hand shot through the window to manually release the lock, and then he opened the door before the driver had time to do much more than swear under his breath.

"Hey, you," he said to the second agent.

The man turned, giving Ethan full view of his

features. He, too, looked to be in his thirties, but his hair was lighter than his partner's, and his expression was more flinty than arrogant. "Satisfied?"

The driver closed the door, snuffing out the interior light. "If I were you, I'd be careful who I piss off. Your visit to Charleston hasn't exactly endeared you to the powers that be."

"Do I look worried?"

Addie's SUV pulled up just then. She got out of her vehicle and hurried over to the car. She was barefoot, too, and still dressed for bed except for the weapon she held at her side. She looked incredibly appealing in the moonlight, hair all tangled and eyes flashing with excitement. "What's going on?"

"These guys are federal agents. They've been watching your house tonight," Ethan said.

Her brows lifted. "Well, that's interesting."

"They claim they don't know anything about the break-in. Didn't see a thing."

"How convenient for them." She leaned in. "What's in the back seat?"

"Nothing, as far as I can tell."

She made sure the agents were aware of her weapon. "Think we can convince them to pop the trunk?"

"Doubtful," Ethan said. "They haven't been very cooperative."

Addie straightened. "Feds." She made it sound

like the lowest form of indictment. She turned to Ethan. "How do we know they didn't do more than just watch my house? We only have their word for it."

The driver shifted his gaze to Addie. "Trust me, Detective, if we wanted to enter your house, you'd never know we were there. We sure as hell wouldn't set off the alarm."

Addie pounced. "Who said anything about an alarm?"

"Good question," Ethan said.

The driver glanced at him. "Still hypothetically speaking?"

"Sure."

"It's a hot night. If we'd been watching Detective Kinsella's house for any length of time, we would have had the windows down to get a cross breeze. We could have heard an alarm without actually seeing anything until the two of you came flying off the porch, armed and in your underwear. Being the conscientious types, we would have circled the block to see if we could figure out what was going on."

"So your hearing is fine, it's just your other senses that are lacking," Addie said.

The agent's gaze dropped appreciatively. "Nothing wrong with my eyesight."

"Hey, eyes up here." Ethan rapped on the hood to attract the agent's attention. "You can tell Gwen

Holloway if she wants to keep track of my where-abouts, she can come find me herself."

"We're not your messengers, Agent Barrow."

"Just beat it," Addie said wearily. "Your sur-veillance has been busted. If you insist on hang-ing around my neighborhood, I'll be forced to haul you in on suspicion."

"That would be a big mistake."

"We'll see, I guess."

"Yes, we will. In the meantime, you two have a good night." The Charger peeled away from the curb, swerving so sharply that Addie and Ethan had to jump back.

Addie swore as they stood, gazing after the car. At the end of the street, the brake lights flashed, and then the driver gunned the engine as he shot around the corner.

She said in awe, "Are you sure those clowns are federal agents? Who teaches you people to drive, anyway?"

"Always a few bad apples," he said.

"No kidding." She pushed back her tousled hair. "You really think they're working for Gwen Hol-loway? How the hell does she still have the kind of clout that she can call up the FBI and order surveillance on another agent?"

"Profiling wasn't her only talent at the Bureau," Ethan said. "She excelled at politics. She made sure that people in power owe her."

Addie shook her head. "I understand how the

system works, but dedicating resources and man-power to protect her reputation seems like over-kill. And I thought I'd seen egos in the police department."

"You have to take into account the current at-mosphere at headquarters. The FBI is still reeling from corruption and bribery charges, and the last thing the brass needs is publicity from a botched investigation and cover-up that wrongly indicted one of the most celebrated profilers since the in-ception of the BAU. Given all that, it's an easy sale for Gwen. One phone call and she's provided all the technical and logistical support she needs to shut us down. But beyond the Bureau's repu-tation and Gwen's ego, something else may be at play here. There's still a lot about Gwen you don't know."

"Then tell me."

He gave her a skeptical look as he rubbed the back of his neck. "Not sure this is the time or place."

"Oh, after that little confrontation, I think this is exactly the time and place."

Ethan glanced around uneasily. "Let's go back to your house, then. I feel like an idiot standing out here in my underwear."

"We need to check the neighborhood first. You can talk while I drive."

He followed her back to the SUV, and they climbed in. Addie started the engine and pulled away from the curb. "Maybe we'll get lucky. Our suspect can't have gotten far on foot."

Ethan nodded, turning to search the shadowy yards as they made the block.

"So tell me about Gwen Holloway," Addie said.

"In a nutshell, she may have more than ego and reputation riding on our investigation."

"So you implied, but that doesn't really tell me anything."

"I think this is personal for her. She has an ax to grind."

"With you?"

"With me, with my father. I never told you this, but he wanted her transferred out of the BAU."

"So she's taking it out on you? Twenty-five years is a long time to carry a secondary grudge," Addie said. "You were just a little kid back then."

He turned to study her profile. "Same age as you when you lost your mother."

She scowled out the windshield. "We both lost a lot. That was a seriously messed-up time."

"Understatement."

She glanced at him before returning her attention to the road. "Go back to Gwen Holloway. How do you know your father wanted her transferred?"

"I overheard an argument between them. My mother and I had come down one weekend to stay with my grandparents. It was in the middle of the Twilight Killer case, and my father had been in Charleston for weeks. That was unusual for a profiler. Despite what you see on TV, they're deskbound most of the time. But for whatever reason, my father wanted to be in on the action, and he worked closely with the task force. He became so consumed with the investigation that he rarely called, let alone visited. I didn't realize until later that my parents' marriage was falling apart. I guess that time was a trial separation. I only knew that things weren't right and that my mother cried a lot. Anyway, on our last night in Charleston, my father left the house to meet Gwen in the garden, and I followed him."

Addie turned a corner and drove half a block before commenting. "You saw them together? *Together*, together?"

"She tried to kiss him. When he pushed her away, she attacked him."

Addie fell silent for another long moment. "Ethan, what are you saying here?"

He scanned the shadows, still searching. "There's a reason Gwen Holloway shut me down ten years ago and why she's still trying to control the narrative even today. Yes, it's about reputation and ego and protecting her business interests, but it's more than that. Like I said, for her, it's personal."

"I get that, but you're still beating around the bush. If you think she had something to do with my mother's murder, just say so."

"All I can tell you is that Gwen was as familiar with the Twilight Killer case as my father. They worked on it together for months. She knew Orson Lee Finch's MO, his signature, his kill list. Everything. She helped develop the profile."

"Means and motive, but what about opportunity?"

"My father was already showing signs of a breakdown. Disorientation, blackouts…" Ethan trailed off as a cloud descended, the same darkness he often experienced when he thought about his father's illness.

"So you think it's possible Gwen killed my mother during one of your father's blackouts and planted his DNA at the crime scene? Then planted his bloody clothing and the murder weapon near his hotel? Just to be clear, that is what you're suggesting, isn't it?"

"It's a theory, nothing more."

Addie made another turn. "The other day, you said the match from Naomi's database search might have been the result of familial DNA. Do you know anything about Gwen's family?"

"She doesn't have any."

"No living parents or siblings?"

"No."

"What about distant relatives? Cousins, aunts, uncles…?"

"I don't know of any."

Addie checked the rearview mirror. "There is another possibility."

"I'm listening."

"Don't tell me you haven't already thought of it," she said. "What if Gwen's relationship with your father resulted in a baby? Could she have kept something like that a secret?"

"It would be difficult for someone in her position, but not impossible."

"She didn't take a leave of absence after your father's incarceration? No hospitals stays or transfers to remote field offices?"

"None that I've been able to uncover."

"Did you ever consider submitting her DNA to see if you get the same match that Naomi did?"

"I've considered it," he admitted. "But even if I managed to get a sample of Gwen's DNA, there are thousands of public databases. I don't know which one Naomi used."

Addie sighed. "It always comes back to her, doesn't it? She was the catalyst for everything that's happened. And we still don't know how any of this connects to the guy who just broke into my house."

"If it connects at all."

She shot him a glance. "I can't decide which is more unsettling—the possibility that Gwen Holloway sent him to harass me or that he's just some random dude with a fixation. Did you get a look at him?"

"He's too smart for that," Ethan said. "He knows enough to keep his face protected. I chased him into your neighbor's backyard, and then he slipped through a hole in the fence and disappeared. Which tells me he's familiarized himself with your neighborhood. He may even live nearby."

"That's a cheery thought." She eased around another corner. The houses in the neighborhood remained dark, the occupants oblivious to their search. "This is a waste of time," she said in frustration. "He's long gone. Or else he found a place to lie low. Not much more we can do tonight. Tomorrow I'll take a look through some of the empty houses. See if he's holed up in one of them. You're right. That could be how he's able to move through the neighborhood so easily." She pulled into her driveway. The front door stood open.

"Did you close the door before you left?" Ethan asked.

"Yes."

"Are you sure?"

"Yes. I remember closing it after I grabbed my car key."

"But you didn't lock it?"

"Not the dead bolt."

They got out and met in the driveway. "I'll take the back," Ethan said.

ADDIE WAITED UNTIL he'd gone through the gate, and then she crossed the yard and went up the front steps, flattening herself against the wall to listen before she stepped into the foyer. The security system was still disarmed. The blinking message seemed to taunt her as she moved across the foyer into the living area. She cleared the kitchen and then moved down the hallway.

A light flickered from the open door of her bedroom. Her hand tightened on the grip of her weapon as she moved steadily forward, clearing the bathroom and then the guest room before she approached her room.

She paused for only a second to listen before she went in, flipping on the light switch so that she could scan every corner. A candle had been lit and placed on her dresser, along with the photo of Sandra Kinsella and the Cutlers. Someone had scrawled *whore* across her mother's face in red marker.

Addie heard a sound in the hall and spun. When Ethan appeared in the doorway, she dropped her weapon to her side. "All clear outside," he said and then noticed the candle. He came into the room and set his gun aside. "What's this?"

"He must have doubled back while we were circling the neighborhood. He came into the house, lit the candle and defaced my mother's photograph." Addie's gaze lifted in frustration. "Who the hell is this guy, Ethan? How can he come and go from my house so easily?"

"That's what we have to find out."

Addie turned back to the dresser and stared into the candle flame with a brooding frown. "I really wanted to believe he was just another fanatic, but the timing can't be coincidental. He first appeared in my backyard right after I met you in White Point Garden. Do you think he was watching me even then?"

"I don't know, Addie."

She picked up the photograph and ran her finger over the ugly word. "If he's connected to the DNA evidence and Naomi's research, then why is he coming after me specifically? Naomi contacted you. You're the one who instigated a new investigation. Not that I want him coming after you," she quickly added. She stared down at her mother's marred face and then handed the photograph to Ethan.

"I recognize the deputy chief," he said. "The other woman is his wife?"

"Yes. You met Helen once years ago."

"Now I remember. It was an awkward encounter. She seemed to be evaluating my every word."

"She's a shrink. Comes with the territory. Plus, she's very protective of me."

Ethan glanced up from the photograph. "The Cutlers and your mother were close?"

"Helen and David have always been like family. I called them aunt and uncle when I was little. I spent more time at their house than I did my own.

My mother was a party girl. She had me when she was young, and I guess she never really grew up."

"She was a beautiful woman," Ethan said.

"Yes, she was." Addie took the photo and propped it against the mirror. All those dear faces seemed almost sinister in the candlelight. "Helen had a really hard time after my mother's death. She not only lost her best friend, but also in a way, she lost me, too. I went to live with my grandmother, and I didn't see her and David as much. My grandmother was protective of me, too. The Cutlers could visit me whenever they liked, but it was a long time before Grandmother would let me spend the night at their house. She never wanted to let me out of her sight."

"Understandable after what happened to her daughter."

At the hands of your father, Addie thought. Or maybe not. "Helen and David did everything they could to stay in touch, but it wasn't the same. Not for a long time."

"You seem close now."

"When my grandmother died, they were there for me. I had no one else. My father was never in the picture. I don't know him or his family. We're strangers that happen to share DNA. I still consider the Cutlers my family. I'm lucky to have them."

"It's interesting how different they all seem," he said with a pensive frown.

"I was just thinking about that earlier. My mother was like a younger, wilder sister to Helen. In some ways, I think Helen lived vicariously through her. Helen was always so down-to-earth. I suppose that's why they got on so well. Opposites attract. She kept my mother grounded." Addie folded her arms around her middle. "That was my favorite photograph of the three of them. Why would someone spoil her image that way?"

"Assuming whoever did this is the same guy you saw earlier, he said that it was time you learn the truth about your mother. Are you sure you don't know what he meant?"

"My mother's past is no secret." Addie bent and blew out the candle. "You say Gwen Holloway's motives are personal—well, so is this. Intensely personal. I hate what he's doing, coming in here and violating my home. This is supposed to be my safe place, my sanctuary, and now I can't even stand to be in my own bedroom."

"You're a cop, Addie. You've seen this before. He's taunting you. Don't let him get under your skin."

"Easier said than done. I'm a cop, yes, but I'm also human. The thought of him going through my things makes my skin crawl. I'm not sleeping in here tonight," she said with a defiant glower.

"You don't have to. Take the spare bedroom. I'll sleep on the couch."

"I'll take the couch, but we can argue over

sleeping arrangements later." She moved to the door. "I could use another drink. Something stronger than beer this time."

"You go ahead," he said. "I'll process the scene. Do you have a print kit in your car?"

"Yes, but you won't find anything. You can bet he wore gloves."

"Probably, but it's worth a shot."

Addic paused in the doorway to glance back at him. "I don't like being on the other side of things."

"I know you don't. But it's okay. We'll figure it out."

Funny how capable and comforting he could seem standing there in nothing but his boxers. Maybe it was the ripple of all those muscles or the memories that were suddenly storming through Addie's head. She felt weak in the knees and tried to convince herself it was nothing but aftershock.

She glanced away then brought her gaze back to him. "It helps that you're here tonight. Thank you for that."

"You don't need to thank me. I'm the one who got you into this."

She shrugged. "Maybe, maybe not. We still don't know if this guy has anything to do with you."

"Regardless, I think we can both agree that I owe you. I made a lot of mistakes ten years ago. I'll always regret how things ended between us."

She rubbed a hand up and down her arm as she scowled into the bedroom. "I don't want to talk about that right now."

"There are still things you need to know about me," he said.

Addie leaned back against the door frame and sighed. "Not now, Ethan, please. It's been a long day. I'm done in. And besides, do you really want to have a serious conversation in your underwear?"

"Not like you have any room to talk."

She smiled. "We must have looked like a pair of lunatics running around the neighborhood like this. Good thing no one saw us. Except for those two idiots in the Charger."

"Yes, they certainly got an eyeful," Ethan agreed. His gazed dropped and lingered admiringly.

"Hey," she said softly. "Eyes up here."

"Can't help myself. You've always had great legs."

"And I thought you were only interested in my mind."

"That, too."

Their gazes locked, and Addie's breath quickened. Strange that the man who had betrayed her and left her brokenhearted could stand half-naked before her and the last thing she wanted was to send him away.

Something must have shifted in her eyes or

in her smile. She hadn't said or done anything, and yet Ethan had picked up on a vibe. His gaze deepened. She could almost hear the throb of his pulse, the sudden rush of his blood. He said nothing, either. Didn't move so much as an inch toward her, and yet Addie was suddenly trembling. Her heart flailed as images bombarded her once more. All those hot nights locked together in the bedroom of her tiny apartment. The long, soulful kisses. The groans and soft cries as he devoured her and then she him.

"I remember how it was, too," he said. "I remember every inch of that little garage apartment. And of you."

"That was a long time ago," Addie felt compelled to remind him.

"You really were something," he said in a hushed voice. "Like a wild colt. All legs and untamed excitement."

"That's how you remember me?" She laughed. "I was a mess. Right out of the academy, uncertain and untested, but trying desperately to prove myself. The best that can be said is that I was exuberantly green."

"You always struck me as supremely confident."

"You took care of that."

He stared at her for the longest moment. "I'm sorry."

She shook her head and turned away. "No,

I'm sorry. I don't know why I said that. I don't know why I keep picking at you." She paused and glanced back at him. "It's easier to guilt someone else than to admit your own screwups."

"You've every right to blame me."

She closed her eyes on a breath. "We've both paid our dues. Anyway, I didn't want to get into anything heavy tonight. We've been through the wringer already. We can talk in the morning."

"If that's what you want."

"Ethan?" She bit her lip. "I'm glad you're here tonight. I said that already, didn't I?"

"I'm not tired of hearing it." He stared at her so intently, Addie felt as if she'd had the wind knocked from her lungs.

She said on a whisper, "Ethan."

"If you keep saying my name like that, I swear I'll—"

"Ethan."

He was across the room in a flash, pulling her against him, pushing up her shirt so that he could splay his hands across her bare skin. Addie returned his kiss with a pent-up ardor that stunned her. She'd been alone and celibate for far too long, and common sense deserted her like a caged bird released unexpectedly into the wild. Her heart pounded. Her blood heated. She didn't know what to do with herself. She didn't know what Ethan expected of her.

Wrapping one arm around his neck, she steadied herself with the other hand flattened against the wall. She pressed into him, needy and demanding and feeling more reckless than she had in years. It was heady, that don't-give-a-damn feeling. An intoxicating mix of lust and freedom.

He kissed her, broke away to nuzzle her neck and then kissed her again. Addie drank him in like a cool glass of water on a hot summer's day. She savored but was nowhere near sated.

"I'd rip your clothes off if you were wearing any," she murmured against his lips.

He laughed softly.

"Kiss me again," she demanded.

He willingly complied, and when he finally drew away, she tried to pull him back to her. "No. Don't go away."

"I think I have to."

She sighed. "Why?"

"Addie, you know why."

"No, I don't. I want this. See? Eyes wide-open."

He cupped her face and dropped his forehead to hers. "What am I going to do with you?"

"Nothing, apparently."

He drew away once more. "You think I like being the spoiler? I want this, too. But those unresolved issues don't just magically go away. You'll regret this in the morning."

"There you go again, thinking you still know me."

"I do know you. No matter how much you try

to pretend otherwise, you haven't forgiven me yet. I don't blame you. I haven't earned back your trust. Maybe I never will. The last thing I ever want to do is hurt you again."

She tugged down her shirt with brisk efficiency. "You're assuming that I'm emotionally invested. People can sleep together just because they want to, you know. It doesn't have to be a big deal."

"For us it does."

"If you say so." She moved toward the hallway. "You go ahead and process the crime scene, Ethan. Take all the time you need. I'll just go have that drink now."

"Addie."

She put up a hand. "Nope. Discussion's over," she said without glancing back.

ADDIE COULDN'T SLEEP. She threw off the covers and rose, treading softly down the hallway so as not to awaken Ethan on the couch. She moved to the window and stared out into the night, her gaze moving from house to house as she searched the shadowy yards.

Ethan stirred behind her. Then he bolted upright as he grabbed for his gun.

"It's just me," she said.

"Addie? What's the matter?"

"I couldn't sleep."

He rose and came over to the window to join her, peering out at the night just as she was.

"He's out there," Addie murmured. "I can feel him watching me."

"We can fix that." Ethan reached over to close the blinds, but she stopped him.

"No, don't. I want him to see me. I want him to know that I'm not scared of him."

"You're taunting him," Ethan said. "Not a good idea."

Addie shrugged. "Drawing him out is the only way we can catch him."

"So you're using yourself as bait."

"Wouldn't be the first time."

He was silent for a moment. "I don't like to think about that."

"Why? We both have dangerous jobs. Don't go all caveman on me, Ethan. I know how to take care of myself."

"I never doubted it. I can still be concerned, can't I?"

"I guess I did give you reason to worry earlier," she admitted grudgingly. "I let him drive me out of my own bedroom. A momentary weakness."

"You're entitled."

"Ethan?"

He turned to study her profile. "What is it, Addie?"

"Do you ever think about what it might have

been like if things hadn't ended the way they did for us?"

"That's an abrupt change of topic," he said in surprise. "I thought you didn't want to get into anything heavy."

She shrugged again. "Just answer the question."

He seemed to consider his response. "What you're really asking is how things might have been different if I hadn't lied to you. I used to think about it all the time."

"And now?"

He stared out the window with a brooding frown. "At some point, I had to move on. But being here with you has brought back a lot of memories."

"For me, too," she admitted. "I think we had something special. Or was I just kidding myself? Was that a lie, too? I never could figure out where your deception began and ended."

"What I felt for you was never a lie. If you believe nothing else, please trust me on that one."

"Maybe it doesn't matter anymore," she said on a wistful note.

"And maybe it does." He put a tentative hand to her cheek. "Addie."

She closed her eyes on a breath. Then tilted her face to his.

The kiss was gentle at first, almost sweetly hesitant. And then as she responded, he threaded his hands through her hair and drew her to him.

Addie clung to him, willing away the past, willing away any negative thought that might once again kill the moment.

She reached up and closed the blinds. Without the soft glow of the security lights, the room fell into darkness. Ethan was barely more than a silhouette as he walked her slowly back to the couch. She sank into the cushions and he hovered over her, staring at her intently before slowly moving down her body, kissing and stroking with fingers and tongue until those ripples of pleasure exploded and she thrust her hands in his hair, tugging him up and over her once more.

She wrapped her legs around him, drawing him in as her eyes closed and her head fell back in ecstasy.

Chapter Twelve

Ethan was already up and dressed the next morning by the time Addie got around. She told him to help himself to anything in the kitchen while she stumbled groggily to the bathroom to shower. When she came out a few minutes later, dressed in her usual jeans and tank, she avoided his gaze as she went about the business of gathering her keys and weapon.

"Are you ready?" she asked as she headed for the door. "I'll take you by your hotel so you can change and then we can go see Vivian DuPriest. If you're still up for it, that is."

"Just drop in on her?"

"Unless you have a better idea. I don't have a phone number, but I know where she lives. My grandmother and I used to walk by her house sometimes. Besides, if we just show up at her door, she'll be less likely to turn us down."

"Then I guess I'm ready."

He went out the front door and waited on the porch while Addie set the alarm and locked up.

"For all the good that dead bolt will do," she muttered. "I'll look for a locksmith this afternoon."

"Addie," Ethan said as they climbed into her vehicle.

She could feel the intensity of his gaze through the lenses of his sunglasses. She pretended to adjust the rearview mirror to escape the impact. "What is it?"

"Should we talk about last night? I don't like this awkwardness between us."

"We'll get over it." She dropped her hand from the mirror and turned to face him. "For what it's worth, you were right about us. I don't have regrets, but maybe it would have been best to keep things professional. We do still have issues, and maybe I haven't forgiven you. I want to. I know it's petty of me to keep harping on the past."

"It's not petty. It's self-preservation. I get it."

She shrugged. "Still, it doesn't say much for my character. This may be presumptuous, but I'm going to say it, anyway. Where can this ever go, Ethan? You live and work in Virginia, and my home is in Charleston. I don't see myself ever leaving this city. I belong here."

"I know that."

"And what I said about hooking up being fine with me...sometimes it is. Sometimes a casual relationship is all I want. But not with you. You were right about that, too. Nothing about us has ever been casual. Or easy, for that matter."

He smiled. "No."

"Things are really complicated right now. The investigation is heating up. Maybe we should just concentrate on that."

"Maybe we should."

She nodded. "We're cool then? Truce still on?"

"Truce is still on."

"Okay. Let's get to work." She started the engine and backed out of the driveway. The neighborhood was just coming awake. She waved to a couple she recognized as they pushed a stroller down the sidewalk. For one split second, she let herself go there. She imagined a different life, one with a husband and kids, playdates and soccer games and noisy evening meals eaten in the dining room rather than at her solitary perch at the bar. She imagined someone to wake up to in the morning and someone to come home to at night. Addie liked her life just fine. She really did. But sometimes she had the passing thought that more might be better.

Shaking off her momentary discontent, she pulled onto King Street, heading south toward the water.

She parked in a lot across the street from Ethan's hotel and got out with him.

"You want to come up?" he asked.

"No, thanks. There's a coffee shop just down that way. I'll get caffeinated while you change. Take your time, though. I'm in no hurry."

"I know the one you mean. I'll meet you there and grab a cup to go," he said.

He leaned in, and despite their previous conversation about keeping things professional, Addie thought he meant to kiss her, just a peck goodbye as if they were an old married couple. Instead, he brushed a leaf from her hair and then he was gone. She watched in bemusement as he crossed the street and disappeared inside the hotel. How could such a light touch electrify so many butterflies in her stomach? How could her world have gone so crazy so quickly?

She turned and headed down the sidewalk toward the coffee shop. The morning was already hot and steamy. She tucked back her damp hair and kept her eyes peeled as she walked along. She didn't want to be caught unaware as she had been the day before. The image of her stalker slipping up behind her flashed in her head, and she turned to glance over her shoulder. Traffic was sparse on the street, and only a few pedestrians were out and about. Addie stopped beneath an awning on the pretext of adjusting her sandal strap. Across the street, someone lurked in a recessed doorway. She could see little more than a silhouette, but she could feel eyes on her. Or was that her imagination?

She continued down the street to the coffee shop, pausing to glance in the plateglass window before entering. If someone had followed her, she couldn't detect him.

Placing her order at the register, she sat down at a window table and faced the door. Her iced coffee arrived a few minutes later, along with a raspberry muffin. She nibbled and sipped as she stared out the window. A tall woman in aviator sunglasses caught her attention. She wore a dark suit and polished loafers, a somber outfit for a summer morning. She'd never met Gwen Holloway in person, but Addie recognized the former profiler from her book jackets and program materials.

She halted on the sidewalk when she saw Addie staring at her through the window. A chill shot through Addie even as she braced herself for the coming confrontation. It was no accident that Gwen Holloway had picked the same coffee shop. She had tailed Addie here, may even have orchestrated the break-in at her home last night. What else did the woman have up her sleeve?

As if sensing and relishing Addie's trepidation, Gwen Holloway smiled and removed her dark glasses as she came into the shop.

Like Addie, she placed her order at the counter. Then she turned and swept her gaze across the tables before lighting once again on Addie. She lingered near the register, but Addie knew it was too much to hope that she'd ordered her coffee to go. Once she had her cup in hand, she made a beeline for Addie's table.

"Detective Kinsella, isn't it? I'm Gwen Holloway." Addie rose and they shook hands. "Mind if I join you?" Before Addie could protest, Gwen pulled out the chair across from her and sat down.

"Of course," Addie said after the fact. "How did you know who I am?"

"I recognized you from the photograph that accompanied your program application. You aroused my curiosity early on."

"How come?"

"It seems you have a lot of fans in the Charleston Police Department. They couldn't say enough good things about you. So I dug a little deeper to see if all the hype was warranted."

"And?"

Gwen gave her a long assessment. "You and your partner have an impressive record. More closed cases than any detectives in your department. You're an impressive team. I'm sure he'll miss you over the next few weeks, but his loss will be this city's gain. The insight and tools you'll acquire from my program will change how you approach police work. You'll be a different investigator by the time the course is concluded. But I warn you, Detective, it won't be a cakewalk. The schedule is demanding."

"I look forward to the challenge."

Gwen smiled as she picked up her coffee. "So

do I." She turned to scan the street before refocusing on Addie. She had something on her mind. That much was obvious. Addie thought about the two agents sent to watch her house last night and Ethan's speculation that Gwen Holloway's interest in their investigation might be motivated by something darker than ego.

Addie had seen photographs of James Merrick. Ethan bore a slight resemblance to his father, but not so much that alarm bells had gone off when she'd first met him or even after she'd fallen in love with him. The truth of his identity had hit her like a sledgehammer blow. But the shock of that revelation was all in the past. Now when she conjured an image of James Merrick, Gwen Holloway was at his side, perhaps plotting his demise. Addie imagined the profiler's growing disenchantment with his protégée, and her rage that everything she'd worked for could so easily be tossed aside. In some ways, Addie sympathized. Times hadn't changed in that regard. Women in law enforcement were still held to a higher standard. They still had to work twice as hard to prove themselves to their male superiors, and second chances came few and far between.

But Addie doubted that Gwen Holloway would appreciate her empathy.

"It's nice to have this chance to chat," Gwen said. "We'll be spending a lot of time together for the next few weeks. It's always good to break the ice."

"How did you know where to find me?" Addie asked.

"I dropped by Ethan's hotel to see him. I saw the two of you drive up."

"So you followed me here?"

"Yes. Is that a problem?"

"It's not a problem. I don't mind breaking the ice," Addie said. "We can chat for as long as you like. But I don't think that's the real reason you're here."

Gwen's eyes glittered with an emotion Addie couldn't define and didn't trust. "You're both perceptive and blunt. I like that."

Addie said nothing.

"Since we both favor the direct approach, I won't beat about the bush. I'm concerned about Ethan's presence here in Charleston. I'm even more worried about his frame of mind."

Addie was immediately on guard. "Why?"

Gwen cradled her cup in both hands as she leaned in. "I know all about your past with Ethan. I know what he did to you. You're more aware than anyone how obsessed he is with clearing his father's name. The evidence against James remains damning, and yet Ethan has convinced himself of his father's innocence. He dragged you into his delusion once before, and it didn't end well for either of you."

Addie took a moment before responding. "With all due respect, how is any of that your concern?"

"I'm concerned for a multitude of reasons."

"Why? As I understand it, Ethan is here on his own time. He's not utilizing FBI resources or manpower to further a personal investigation. He's working alone with a little help from me. But even if that wasn't the case, you don't work for the Bureau. Why do you care what he does?"

Annoyance flashed across Gwen's features before she shrugged it away. "I don't know how much Ethan has told you about our background, but we go way back. I knew him when he was just a little boy."

"Yes, I know. His father was your mentor," Addie said. "I've read all your books. I found them fascinating, and I don't say that to suck up."

"That's not your style, is it, Detective Kinsella? You're fiercely independent. You don't like giving or receiving favors, and as I noted earlier, you're blunt. I appreciate that. So let me be straight with you. Unless you cut Ethan Barrow off at the knees, that man will be your downfall. I know what I'm talking about."

Addie frowned. "What do you think he'll do to me?"

"The same thing he did before, only worse. The same thing his father tried to do to me."

"Which was...?"

Gwen glanced around, automatically scoping

out their surroundings. "It may surprise you to know that I've remained good friends with Ethan's mother and stepfather over the years. And with Ethan when he would allow it. I've watched his career successes—and his failures—with great interest. I've always known he had something special—intelligence, talent, dedication, but also that indefinable quality that sets certain agents apart from the pack. He's like his father in that respect. He has James's insight and instincts. His single-mindedness. He could truly be one of the greats. The powers-that-be want him in the BAU, but Ethan is nothing if not stubborn. His resistance hasn't gone unnoticed."

"What does that have to do with my downfall?" Addie asked.

"If he's so careless with his own career, I can't imagine that he'll have much regard for yours. He's a man on a mission, Detective Kinsella, and he won't stop until he takes you down with him. He reminds me more and more of James with each passing day."

"From what I've read, a lot of factors contributed to James Merrick's breakdown. Ethan may be driven, but there is nothing wrong with his head."

An unpleasant smile flitted. "Are you sure about that? When I first knew James, I would have sworn he was as steady as you or I. There were aspects of his personality and behavior that troubled me, but I told myself he was just unconventional, as so many brilliant people are. I tried to convince myself of his eccentricity right up until the moment your mother was murdered because James Merrick could no longer distinguish between fantasy and reality. He became Orson Lee Finch that night, the killer he had hunted so intently for months. Looking back, I saw the signs. I've always wondered, if I'd spoken up earlier, could I have stopped him? Maybe your mother would still be alive."

Oh, she was good, Addie thought. So good that she could almost make Addie believe she had her best interests at heart. Gwen Holloway spoke as if they were confidantes. A sage imparting her wisdom. *Listen to me. Learn from my mistakes with Ethan's father.*

Addie knew exactly what the woman was doing. She recognized Gwen's cunning and manipulation, and yet a part of her couldn't help asking, "What signs?"

"I don't know if I can explain it so that you'll understand, but James became someone else when he worked a case. He was obsessed, yes. We all were. But it was more than that. He lived and breathed the kills until he became the shadow of whatever monster we hunted. He had instincts and insight like no one I've ever seen before or since, although Ethan comes close. When James lost himself in the hunt, nothing else mattered to him. Not rules, not protocol, not even his family. Does that sound like anyone else you know?"

Addie's hackles rose in defense. "It sounds nothing like Ethan."

"Then you're lying to yourself just as I did all those years ago."

"You underestimate me." Addie scooted back her chair and stood. "My eyes are wide-open. I know exactly what I'm getting into. I'll help Ethan for as long and as much as I want and then I'll walk away."

"Easier said than done, Detective."

"Maybe. But here's where you and I differ. I don't expect anything in return. I certainly would never want anyone to leave a wife and child for me."

Fire flashed in Gwen Holloway's eyes, a quick, violent flare that took Addie's breath away. Then just like that, the blaze went out and the woman stared up at Addie with cool resolve. "You're out of line, Detective."

"Then I apologize. But you're the one who followed me in here. You're the one who started this conversation. You said you appreciate my candor, so here it is. My relationship with Ethan is none of your business. What we do on our own time is none of your business. I realize that speaking my mind will likely jeopardize my standing in your program, but I won't be manipulated. And I won't be used as a weapon against Ethan." Addie started to walk away and then turned back to the table. "Oh. And tell those two agents you sent to watch my house last night to knock it off. All you're doing is making me wonder why you're so desperate to stop Ethan's investigation."

Gwen rose. "You don't want me for an enemy."

"No, I don't," Addie agreed. "But if you start a war, you'll find I'm no pushover. Unless I get word that I've been dismissed from your program, I'll see you first thing tomorrow morning."

She walked outside and put on her sunglasses. Ethan was just crossing the street. She strode over to him. His gaze went past her to the coffee shop, and he muttered something under his breath.

"What happened in there?"

Addie shrugged. "You were right about her. She's manipulative and vindictive. And unless I miss my guess, she's hiding something."

"What did she say to you? Or maybe I should ask what you said to her."

Addie shrugged again. "Suffice to say, she's not my biggest fan."

Ethan grinned. "That's okay. I am."

Chapter Thirteen

Addie parked near Waterfront Park, and they walked down the Battery to the farthest point of the peninsula. Crossing East Bay, they lingered in the gardens while she recounted her conversation with Gwen Holloway and the insinuation that Ethan might be following in his father's tragic footsteps. He didn't seem at all surprised. "That sounds like her," he said with a shrug and then wondered aloud about the best way of approaching Vivian DuPriest. In the end he agreed that showing up at her house was their only recourse. Addie wasn't surprised by the leap. Changing the subject kept them both from dwelling on Gwen's insidious implications.

"Remember, we've got history and name recognition on our side," she said. "Vivian was a reporter assigned to the Twilight Killer investigation, and she planned to write a book about the case. She may be a recluse now, but I don't think she'll be able to resist seeing us."

They walked through the park, past the cannons and gazebo to Meeting Street, and then cut over to Tradd. The houses here were centuries old with hidden courtyards tucked away behind wrought iron gates and layers of shady piazzas overlooking lavish gardens. For the longest time, they strolled in silence, watching their step on the cracked sidewalks. The morning was quiet and peaceful. A breeze stirred luscious perfumes from behind brick walls. A horse-drawn carriage clopped by on the street.

Addie told herself not to be lulled. Even in paradise, danger lurked. The historic district had been Orson Lee Finch's hunting ground. Most of his victims had come from South of Broad, though Addie's mother had grown up north of Calhoun. Ethan's grandparents had lived only a few blocks away. It seemed strange to think that their paths may have crossed when they were children.

"What's the house number?" Ethan asked. "We must be getting close."

"Yes, this is it." She pointed across the street to a three-story dark brick home with hunter green shutters.

Ethan whistled. "Ida McFall wasn't kidding about old money."

"The DuPriests go back a long way in this city," Addie said. "My grandmother knew the family slightly, though they hardly moved in the same circles. And of course, she became one of Vivian's most avid readers." They crossed the street, and Addie tried the gate. It swung inward with barely a squeak. "Must be a sign. Maybe she'll see us, after all."

The scent of jasmine trailed them to a side door, which was the main entrance on many of the old homes. Ethan rang the bell, and after a moment, a twentysomething man in khakis and a blue knit shirt the exact shade of his eyes answered. Their appearance seemed to confuse him. He glanced past them to the street as if he had been expecting someone else.

"Can I help y'all?" he drawled.

"We'd like to see Vivian DuPriest," Addie said.

"Honey, you and a few dozen other people." He gave them a reproving once-over. "I handle her schedule, so I know she's not expecting anyone. If y'all are here to get a book signed or you want an interview, I'm afraid you're barking up the wrong tree. She doesn't do speaking engagements, either, nor is she interested in joining your book club. If you have other business, then I suggest you make an appointment."

Ethan took out his credentials. "I'm Special Agent Ethan Barrow with the FBI, and this is Detective Adaline Kinsella with the Charleston PD. We're here on a matter of some urgency."

The man scanned their IDs and then glanced up with a puzzled frown. "I don't understand. Is this about her niece's accident? She's already spoken to the police."

Ethan put away his credentials. "Tell her James Merrick's son would like to speak with her."

"And Sandra Kinsella's daughter," Addie said. "Please make sure you get those names right. Trust me, she'll want to see us."

The young man looked simultaneously annoyed and intrigued by their insistence. "Wait here."

He closed the door in their faces, and Addie exchanged a glance with Ethan. "He'll be back."

"We'll see."

The man returned a few minutes later and motioned them into a spacious foyer with paneled walls and marble floors. From there he led them down a wide hallway lined with gilt mirrors and family portraits. The house was beautifully appointed but dark and oppressive. Addie was glad when they were ushered into a garden room, where sunlight poured in through skylights. The effect was almost blinding after the dim hallway, and it took a moment to adjust to the brilliance. A wall of French doors looked out on a tropical wonderland of hibiscus, ginger and hummingbird trees.

Vivian DuPriest looked anything but traditional. Little wonder she had gravitated to the most dazzling room in the house, Addie thought. Her vivid red hair and turquoise kimono rivaled the showiness of her garden. She looked to be in her early sixties, petite but hardly fragile. She watched with avid curiosity as they came into the room, but she didn't rise to greet them.

"Thank you for agreeing to see us," Addie said.

The woman looked her up and down. "So you're Sandra Kinsella's daughter." She turned her attention to Ethan. "And you're James Merrick's son. You were children the last time I saw you. And look at you now. A police detective and an FBI agent. How interesting that you've both chosen careers in law enforcement. How intriguing that you've come here together. Would you like tea?"

Addie exchanged another glance with Ethan. "We're fine, thank you."

Vivian waved to a pair of wicker chairs with high backs and curved arms. "At least sit. I don't like lurkers."

They sat across from the sofa where she perched.

She picked up a floral teacup and sipped delicately as her gaze vectored back in on Ethan. "You look like James. I can see his kindness in your smile and his drive in your eyes. I sense something darker there, too, I think." She took another sip of her tea. "Your father was a very brilliant man."

"Did you know him well?" Ethan asked.

"Well enough, I suppose. I had the distinction of being the only reporter ever allowed to interview the great James Merrick. We got along well. I respected his boundaries, and he appreciated my discretion. And we both enjoyed a good scotch. I rarely leave my home these days, but when I still had a license, I would drive to the state capital to visit him now and then." She smiled as she regarded Ethan thoughtfully. "I see that surprises you."

"It does," he admitted. "Until recently, I was under the impression that I was my father's only visitor."

"Oh, I'm sure a great many people have gone to see James over the years. He is still a source of endless fascination. Whether he received any of those visitors is another question."

"But he agreed to see you," Ethan said.

"Yes. As I said, we always got on. I even tried to smuggle in a bottle of Johnnie Walker Blue once, but it was confiscated at the desk, more's the pity."

"Was he responsive when you saw him?"

"I suppose that depends on your definition."

Addie turned to glance at Ethan's profile. His arms rested on the curve of the chair, and he leaned forward slightly as if he were hanging on Vivian DuPriest's every word. She would appreciate that, but he wasn't faking interest to flatter her. He was hungry to hear about his father.

Something in his voice, the barest hint of hope, made Addie want to reach out to him. Not for the first time, she wondered what it must have been like for him as a child and then as an adolescent, living in the shadow of his father's guilt and desperately wanting to believe in his innocence. Addie's own childhood had been tragic. Losing her mother so violently had been devastating, and it had changed her in ways she would never fully understand. But Ethan's loss might have been harder to accept. Harder to live with, too.

Her gaze shifted to Vivian DuPriest. The woman was something of an enigma. On the surface, she seemed like an aging, eccentric Southern belle, but Addie suspected that was only one of her many personae. Beneath the rouged cheeks and ruby lips, the hardness of a once crack reporter still glimmered through.

Idly, she stirred her tea as she continued to ponder Ethan's question. "James never spoke to me when we visited. I did all the talking. He spent most of our time together looking out the window. He didn't have much of a view, but he seemed captivated by it nonetheless. I used to wonder what he was thinking. His eyes even then were so expressive. Was he responsive?" she mused to herself. "No, not in the way you mean. But I always had the sense that he knew who I was. And I think there was a part of him, some small corner of his consciousness, that remained fully engaged in my chitchat."

"When was the last time you saw him?" Ethan asked.

"Oh, it's been years. I can't even remember

the last time. So many things have happened…"
She trailed away on a wistful note. "It may sound
strange considering his situation, but I wouldn't
want him to see me as I am now. I was always
so strong and resourceful. He admired that about
me."

"I'm sure he did."

"I admired him, too. Such an intensely complicated man, your father. Handsome, too, and
surprisingly charming when he wanted to be. It
pains me the way we are now. Each of us a mere
shell of our former self." She sighed. "I always
wondered about his breakdown."

Ethan's voice sharpened. "What was there to
wonder about?"

Vivian turned to stare out at the garden. A
butterfly flitted over a yellow hibiscus, and she
seemed momentarily transfixed. Then she rallied
with a shrug. "I always prided myself on my per-
ception. That was one of the things that set me
apart as a reporter. I could read people so well.
James's illness happened suddenly, and it mani-
fested so violently. I never saw it coming."

"I don't know about sudden," Ethan said. "My
mother told me that he had been seeing a therapist. He never told anyone else because of his job.
He also consulted a neurologist, but no one could
find the cause of his headaches and blackouts."

"You never told me that," Addie said.

Ethan glanced at her. "I only found out recently. But it doesn't change anything."

Addie lifted a brow. "I disagree, but we can discuss it later."

Vivian DuPriest watched them curiously, her gaze going from one to the other. "Oh, don't mind me. I'm just sitting here wondering what brought the two of you together. And why you've really come to see me."

"We'd like to talk to you about your niece," Addie said. "Naomi Quinlan."

Vivian leaned forward and topped off her teacup. "I've already spoken to the police. I don't know what more I can tell you."

"Detective Yates came to see you?"

"I don't know any Detective Yates," she said with a dismissive wave. "The deputy chief came to see me."

Addie stared at her for a moment. "David Cutler came to interview you?"

"*Interview* sounds too official. He came to pay me a courtesy call. Now you seem surprised, Detective Kinsella, but I don't know why you would be. Charleston is like a small town. Everyone knows everyone. The deputy chief and I go back a long way. Why wouldn't he come to see me in person rather than send one of his detectives?"

Something in the woman's tone, a flicker in her eyes brought Addie to the edge of her seat. Like

Gwen Holloway earlier, what Vivian DuPriest said was not precisely what she meant.

Ethan must have caught the inflection, too. "You say you go back a long way. Did you become acquainted during the Twilight Killer case?"

"We go back even further than that, if you can imagine such a thing. I knew David Cutler when he was still a rookie. He was a good-looking young man and so very ambitious." She eyed them sagely over the rim of her cup. "He went out of his way to assure me that Naomi's death was a tragic accident, so I can't imagine why you would need to talk to me again. Unless, of course, the driver of the car that struck her has been found."

Addie shook her head. "No, not yet, I'm afraid."

Vivian's gaze flicked from one to the other. "Then why don't you tell me what this is really about?"

"We just want to ask you a few questions," Addie said. "We're trying to tie up some loose ends. Naomi's neighbor told us that you and your niece recently had a falling-out."

"By neighbor, I assume you mean Ida McFall. That woman is a terrible busybody, always has been. What else has she told you about me?"

"She said the two of you also go way back."

"Ah, did she? I suppose she mentioned the letters."

"She did, and we would love to hear more about them, but right now we're interested in your relationship with your niece. Ida implied you were upset with Naomi because of a book she was writing."

"I was upset with Naomi because she stole from me. The girl was a thief, plain and simple. I caught her red-handed, so I kicked her out."

"What did she steal?" Addie asked.

"Notes, interviews, research materials. She even pilfered the first draft of my manuscript. She planned to tweak it a bit and pass it off as her own. And after everything I did for her. I brought her into my home when she had nowhere else to go, gave her work, a purpose in life, and that's how she planned to repay me. By stealing my legacy."

"You obviously have strong feelings about Naomi," Addie said.

"Why wouldn't I? I inherited money, but I earned my writing credentials by working hard and paying my dues. And yes, I do realize that my passion makes me somewhat suspect, but I didn't run down poor Naomi. As I said, I rarely leave my house these days, and the deputy chief *assured* me that her death was an accident. But your visit suggests otherwise."

"It's an ongoing investigation," Addie said.

"I see."

"Could you tell us what was included in your research materials?" Ethan asked. "Crime-scene photos, autopsy reports…?" He left the question hanging.

"All of the above. Back in those days, I was

well connected. I would sometimes receive a copy of the autopsy report and toxicology screen before they were even sent to the detective on the case. I know what you're thinking," she said as she settled more deeply into the sofa. "But I never betrayed my sources, nor did I use information until I was authorized to do so. Despite my extensive contacts, I never compromised a single investigation."

"Were you assigned to my mother's case?" Addie asked.

"I was assigned to all the major cases. The Twilight Killer investigation took a toll, but your mother's murder was especially troubling. We all thought the killings were over, and then another victim turned up. And to later find out that someone I admired and respected had been accused of such a gruesome crime. I can't imagine what your family went through," she said to Addie. "I knew your grandmother in passing. We belonged to the same garden club for a time. A lovely woman. I was sorry to come across her obituary in the paper."

"Thank you," Addie said. "Were you given a copy of my mother's autopsy report?"

"No, and that was unusual. My contacts knew they could trust me, but from the start, that investigation took a strange turn. There was a complete information blackout. It was as if my sources were afraid to talk me."

"Why would they be afraid?"

"Perhaps their jobs had been threatened. I don't know. I was never given or shown a copy of your mother's autopsy report, but I was fed certain tidbits under the table." She spoke carefully, as if she were gauging Addie's reaction.

"Someone told you that she was pregnant, didn't they?"

Her brow furrowed. "It was only a rumor. I didn't print it because I couldn't corroborate the information. No one would comment on the record. I could barely get anyone to talk off the record. I always wondered why the investigation operated in such secrecy. And why so many of the case files were sealed so quickly."

"You must have a theory," Ethan said.

Vivian glanced at him. "I never thought James committed that murder. No matter his frame of mind, violence wasn't in him." She turned back to Addie. "I've always believed the key to solving your mother's murder was hidden in her unborn baby's DNA. Find the father, find the killer."

Addie's heart thudded. She had the sudden urge to rush out of the room and leave the rest of Vivian DuPriest's story untold. "I don't know what to say to that. I don't know if I believe it."

Vivian's gaze darkened. "Why do you think I was attacked and beaten so viciously? I was on the trail of the truth. I would have uncovered everything eventually. But my recovery took a toll, physically and mentally. For nearly a year, I couldn't walk. I couldn't feed or bathe myself. It was a humbling and humiliating experience."

"You don't know who attacked you?" Addie asked.

"I was completely blindsided. Knocked unconscious and left for dead. It's a miracle I'm alive. Like your mother's murder, the investigation surrounding my attack was shrouded in secrecy. I always felt someone with clout was pulling strings. Maybe in the police department, maybe in the FBI. I had enemies in both camps. After James was sent away, no one wanted the truth to come out."

"A third person's DNA was found at the scene of Sandra Kinsella's murder," Ethan said. "That person was never identified. Two weeks before your niece's death, she emailed me to say that she'd sent a sample of that DNA to a public database and had gotten a hit. She insisted that I come to Charleston so that we could speak in person. But before I could arrange my schedule, she was killed in the hit-and-run."

"You don't say," Vivian said.

Ethan watched her for a moment. "So you already knew about the DNA results. Naomi stole that sample from you, didn't she?"

"I won't comment about the sample or how and when it was acquired. Naomi was a genealogist. Naturally such a mystery would appeal to her. She came to me with the results. I'm sure I must have been a last resort after everything she'd done, but she was stymied. She'd made contact, she said. She and the donor had emailed back and forth, and she'd found out his name and address, but she couldn't connect him to the murder or even to the Twilight Killer case in general. I did some digging and called in a few favors, but the man was a ghost."

"Could you share his name with us?" Addie asked. "Maybe the two of us can find out something."

Vivian hesitated. "You should know that Naomi was struck down by that car only a few days after she came to see me."

"You don't think the hit-and-run was an accident, do you?" Ethan asked.

"I was *assured* that it was."

He glanced at Addie even as he addressed his question to Vivian. "Did you tell David Cutler about Naomi's research?"

Vivian leaned forward and removed the lid from a porcelain box on the coffee table. She took out a slip of paper and handed it to Addie. "I told the deputy chief what he wanted to hear. What I needed him to hear. Naomi led a quiet, mundane life. There was no reason in the world that anyone would want to harm her. Or me, for that matter."

Chapter Fourteen

"That was an interesting visit," Addie said as they headed back to her car. She handed Ethan the folded paper. "We now have a name and address, which is a lot more than we had an hour ago. Although according to Vivian, he's a ghost, so we'll have to do some digging."

"I'll run the name through our databases and see what I can come up with," Ethan said as he glanced down at the name and address. "Daniel Roby. Doesn't ring a bell for me."

"For me, either. Let's go check out that address. Maybe after we talk to him, we'll have some answers."

"I appreciate your enthusiasm, but we need to play this smart," Ethan said. "If we barge in and start asking a lot of questions, we could spook him. I'm guessing the reason he's a ghost is because he has something to hide. Whether it has anything to do with the DNA results remains to be seen, but anyone that low profile usually has a sketchy background. Daniel Roby may not even be his real name."

"What do you suggest we do then?"

"We watch him. We stake out his place. See where he goes, where he works, if he has any visitors. We find out all we can about him before we tip our hand."

Addie glanced up with a frown. "Stake out his place for how long?"

"For as long as it takes. A few days. A week, maybe."

She grimaced. "A week? Ugh. No. I don't have that kind of time to devote to a stakeout, and besides, I hate surveillance. I vote the direct approach."

"Let's compromise," Ethan said. "We watch his place for the rest of the day and then we play it by ear."

"Agreed." She used her remote to unlock her vehicle and then slid behind the wheel while Ethan went around to climb in on the other side. "Let me see that address again." He handed her the paper and she nodded. "Yeah, I know where that street is. It's in Westside before you get to the Citadel." She glanced up at the buzzing vibration of a cell phone.

"Not mine," Ethan said.

"I didn't have time to get a burner, so I left mine in the glove box." She leaned over and extracted the phone, then frowned as she checked her missed calls. "Helen called three times while we were gone." Alarmed, she pressed the play button on her messages and lifted the phone to her ear. "Oh, no."

"What is it?"

She glanced at him as she listened. "David was rushed to the hospital this morning. They think he had a heart attack."

"What's his condition?"

Addie shook her head. "I don't know. Helen says they're running tests." She listened to another message before putting the phone away. "She sounds frantic. I'm sorry, but I have to get to the hospital."

"Yeah, of course. You need me to drive you?"

"No, I'm fine. Sorry about bailing on our surveillance."

"Don't worry about it. I turned in my rental, but I can get another. It's better if we don't use your vehicle for surveillance, anyway."

She nodded. "You'll call me if you find out anything?"

"I'll keep you posted. And you call me if there's any news, okay?"

"I will."

He opened the door to get out and then glanced back. "It'll be okay, Addie. He's a strong guy. Stubborn, too."

"I know. It's just…when I saw him yesterday, I remember thinking how old he looked, and that surprised me. I'd never thought so before. He always seemed so timeless. I never expected this."

"You'll feel better after you see him," Ethan said. "Just be careful, okay? Keep your guard up even while you're at the hospital."

"You, too. Ethan?"

"Yes?"

She bit her lip. "Nothing. I'll see you soon."

She watched him in the rearview mirror as she pulled away from the curb. He kept his gaze on her, too. It was as if neither of them wanted to be the first to break eye contact. As if this might be the last time they were together.

Which was crazy. These were dangerous times, but she and Ethan knew how to take care of themselves. Everything would be fine.

She repeated that sentiment as she drove to the hospital and then as she rode the elevator up to the sixth floor. She exited the lift and glanced around for a moment to get her bearings. A man came down the hallway toward her. He was dressed casually in jeans and a T-shirt with a baseball cap pulled low over his features. He was average height, average build...

Addie was so preoccupied with worry that she barely paid him any mind. Only after he had passed her in they hallway did she turn for a second glance. He had stepped onto the elevator, and his head was bowed as he pushed the button. She could only see the lower part of his face, but Addie could have sworn she saw a grin flash.

Her mind went back to the alley and to the moment when she and her stalker had come face-to-face. Then as now she'd only glimpsed his lower face, but she couldn't forget that sneer.

Her heart thudded and she stood staring at the closed elevator doors for the longest time until she heard someone call her name. She turned to find Helen hurrying toward her.

"Thank goodness you're here, Addie. I was so worried when I couldn't reach you."

"I'm sorry. I didn't have my phone with me. I only got your messages a few minutes ago."

"That's not like you," Helen said. "I'm the one who misplaces phones."

"I didn't misplace it. I just didn't have it with me. Not that it matters. How's David?"

"They've taken him downstairs for more tests." She looped her arm through Addie's and guided her to a quiet bench. "His room is just down that way. We'll see them when they bring him back up."

"Have they told you anything?"

"The preliminary tests look good. They don't think it's his heart, after all. It's more than likely stress related. He may have had a panic attack."

"That doesn't sound like David. He's usually a rock."

Helen frowned. "He's so strong that I sometimes think we forget he's human. So does he. He just keeps pushing himself. He refuses to acknowledge that we're not as young as we used to be. When this is all over, we're making some changes. I know people always say that in a crisis, but I mean it. I won't lose him," she said fiercely.

"You're not going to lose him," Addie said. "If it's stress related, then maybe this will turn out to be a blessing in disguise. You've wanted him to cut back his hours for ages. Maybe this will finally be the catalyst."

"I'll need you on my side," Helen said.

"I'm always on your side."

She let out a long breath. "Do you have any idea how glad I am to see you?"

"I'm sorry I wasn't here earlier. And I'm sorry if I caused *you* stress."

"You're here now. That's all that matters." Helen studied her for a moment. "Are you okay?"

"Yes, of course. Why wouldn't I be?"

"I can always tell when something is bothering you."

"It's not important."

"If it's bothering you, then it's important," Helen said. "What's going on?"

Addie hesitated. "I really didn't want to get into this right now. You've enough on your mind. But I know you'll keep badgering me until I tell you, so…" She trailed off. "Someone tried to break into my house last night."

Helen stared at her in shock. "What? Did you call the police?"

"I am the police, remember?"

Helen's tone turned reproachful. "You know what I mean. Did you file an official report?"

"I haven't had a chance. I've been busy with other things, but we don't need to worry about that right now. I would like to ask you something, though."

"Of course. Anything."

"Remember the other day when you told me you'd lost your phone? Did you ever find it?"

Something flickered in Helen's eyes before she glanced away. "Yes, as a matter of fact, it was underneath the desk in my office. I must have knocked it off without realizing it."

"Is it possible someone took it without you knowing and then returned it?"

"I can't imagine such a thing. Who would steal a phone and then return it?"

"Someone who wanted to get information from it," Addie said.

"What information?"

"You and I texted back and forth before I left on vacation. I reminded you of the alarm code and where you could find the extra key. All of that information was right there in our text messages."

"How would anyone else know about that? And besides, I keep my phone locked just as a precaution against that very thing." Her gaze met Addie's. "There's something you're not telling me. Why on earth would you think someone had gotten your information from my phone?"

"I'm just trying to figure out how this person came by a key to my front door and possibly the code to my security system. The alarm went off last night after I'd changed the code. But night before last, I could have sworn someone had been in my house without setting off the alarm. That would only be possible if the person knew the code."

Helen put a hand on Addie's arm. "You're scaring me with all this talk. Someone came into your house while you were asleep? Are you sure?"

"I'm sure about last night. We caught a glimpse of the suspect as he cut through my neighbor's backyard."

"We?"

"Ethan Barrow was there."

"Oh, Addie."

"I know what you're thinking, but you don't need to worry about me," Addie said. "I know how to take care of myself."

Helen lifted her hand to Addie's cheek. "I know you do, but I'll always worry about you, sweet girl."

"Let's just focus on David right now."

Helen tensed. "We don't need to mention this to him. You know how he feels about Ethan. His blood pressure is through the roof as it is."

"I won't say anything."

"There he is." Helen rose and squared her shoulders. She took a breath and pasted a smile on her face. "How do I look?"

"Beautiful," Addie said.

But her mind was still on their conversation and the term of endearment that Helen had used. No one but Sandra Kinsella had ever called Addie *sweet girl*.

ADDIE SPENT MOST of the day at the hospital, only leaving for a short time to have the locks changed on her doors and then returning to relieve Helen while she went home to rest. David dozed for most of the day. When he awakened, he stared out the window, saying very little to Helen or Addie, but he looked as if he had the weight of the world on his shoulders.

Intermittently, Addie received text messages from Ethan. He had parked down the street from the subject's house but hadn't seen anyone coming or going for hours.

How are things at the hospital?

Fine. David is sleeping. Helen is reading. I may slip out of here soon. I hate hospitals. Even a stakeout is preferable.

Let me know if you're coming. I'll watch for you.

Okay.

Have to go now. Someone just pulled up in the driveway. I'll see if I can get a closer look.

Be careful, Ethan.

"Who are you texting?" Helen asked.

Addie slipped the phone in her pocket as she glanced up. "A friend."

Helen's lips thinned. "A friend, huh? I'll bet."

David said weakly, "Did I miss something? What is going on with you two?"

"Nothing, dear. I'm just giving Addie a hard time."

"Well, don't," he said. "What would our lives be without her?"

"I shudder to think," Helen murmured.

Addie went to his bedside. "How are you feeling?"

He tried to muster a smile. "Cranky. I hate hospitals."

"I know. So do I."

"Then go home," he said firmly. "You've got a big day tomorrow, and there's no point in both of you staying. I wish Helen would go home, too. I don't need a babysitter."

"Well, that's too bad, because you're stuck with me." Helen moved to the other side of his bed. "So long as you're in here, I'm not leaving your side. Not tonight, not ever."

David's gaze turned solemn. "We've been through a lot together, Helen."

"Yes, we have, dear."

He took her hand, entwining his fingers with hers. "I thought I was going to die this morning. So many things went through my head. There's so much I need to say to both of you."

"Shush. We don't need to talk about any of that right now," Helen said.

"Helen—"

"Please, David, not now." Her voice came out sharper than she had undoubtedly meant it. "You need your rest, and we don't need to upset Addie with all this talk about dying."

"Addie?" He said her name as if he'd forgotten about her presence.

"I'm right here, David."

"Your mother loved you very much. You need to know that."

"David, *hush*. You're working yourself up into a state, and the doctor said you need to remain calm." Helen glanced across the bed at Addie. "Would you mind giving us a moment alone?"

"No, of course not. I'll be right outside if you need me."

She moved toward the door, pausing for a moment to glance back over her shoulder. Helen was leaning over the bed, speaking to David in a low voice as she gripped his hand. He turned his head, and for one brief moment, his gaze met Addie's before she slipped out the door.

Her phone rang as she headed down the hallway toward the waiting room. She glanced around as she answered. "Hello?"

"It's Ethan."

"Are you okay? What's going on?"

"I'm sending you a photo I just snapped of Daniel Roby. At least I think that's who he is. He went inside the house about an hour ago, and now he's just come back out again. I'm going to have a look around."

"I don't think that's a good idea," Addie said. "What did you tell me earlier? We need to gather as much information as we can on this guy before we tip our hand."

"I'll be in and out before anyone knows I'm around."

"Ethan, don't do that. I'm just down the street from you. I can be there in ten minutes. Don't do anything without backup. You know that's what you'd tell me."

He laughed softly. "Probably. And you'd do exactly as I'm doing. Don't worry, Addie. I'll be careful. Did the text come through?"

"I'm looking at the photo now." She switched to the text window. "His head is turned away from the camera. I can barely see him."

"Sorry. That was the best I could do. Hang on.

I think I've found a way in. I'll call you back in a minute."

"No, Ethan! Wait for me."

The call went dead. She swore under her breath as she walked over to the window to study the photo. She couldn't see the man's features, but she recognized the clothing and the ball cap pulled over his face. He was the man who had gotten on the elevator behind her.

The phone buzzed, and she jumped. "Ethan?"

"Addie?" His voice sounded strained. "You have to see this place. He's blown up the crime-scene photos and plastered them all over his walls. And there's trash all over the place just like in Naomi's attic. He must have felt the need to hide out there for a while. Or else he was looking for something. The DNA sample most likely."

"If that's true, you need to get out of there before he comes back," Addie said.

"He's got pictures of you, too, Addie. He's your stalker."

Her heart thudded. "Who is he? How does he know me?"

"Whoever he is, he's obviously been watching you for a long time. I'm sending you more images."

"Ethan, the first photograph you sent me. I think I saw him at the hospital this morning. I was just getting off the elevator. But that doesn't make any sense. How would he know I would be here?"

She heard a muffled voice in the background, a crash, and then the call dropped.

"Ethan? Are you there? What happened? Ethan?"

"Is something wrong?" Helen had come up behind her.

Addie whirled. "I don't know. I lost the connection."

Helen frowned. "Was that Ethan Barrow on the phone just now? Where is he? Did something happen?"

"That's what I'm trying to find out. I have to go, Helen. I'll be back as quickly as I can."

"Yes, of course," Helen said. "I'll take care of everything here."

Chapter Fifteen

Addie parked down the street from the address that Vivian DuPriest had given them. Since she didn't know what kind of car Ethan had rented, she had no way of knowing whether his was among the vehicles lined up along the curb. She sat for a moment taking stock of her surroundings. The houses in the neighborhood were small, single-story cottages that had seen better days. College students gravitated to the area because of the rent and the proximity to MUSC. Someone wanting to keep a low profile wouldn't attract much attention with the high turnover in renters.

Addie hoped that she had overreacted to Ethan's dropped call, but she'd tried to reach him a half dozen times on the short trip from the hospital. Something was wrong. She could feel it in her gut.

Exiting the vehicle, she slipped her weapon in the small bag she wore across her body. Then she headed down the sidewalk, glancing over her shoulder to make certain she wasn't followed. She'd texted the address to Matt, and common sense told her she should wait for her partner. But if Ethan was in trouble, timing could be everything.

She checked the front entrance and then circled the house. The back door stood ajar. She went up the steps and glanced through the crack. Drawing her weapon, she toed open the door and entered quickly, clearing each room before moving on to the next.

As she eased into the front room, her gaze lit on the giant photographs pinned to the walls. Slowly, she moved about the room scanning the macabre gallery. Her gaze went to the crime-scene photos first and then to the wall that had been devoted exclusively to her. She had been captured at the lake, at police headquarters, even coming out of her house. Every facet of her life displayed on a madman's canvas.

The creak of a floorboard alerted her to danger, and she whirled. Helen had come in the back way behind her. She stood just inside the room gazing at the disturbing images.

"My God," she whispered.

Addie lowered her weapon. "Helen, what are you doing here?"

"I knew you were in trouble, so I followed you."

Addie started across the room toward her. "That was a foolish thing to do. We need to get you out of here."

"What is this place?" Helen moved to the wall

of crime-scene photos, lifting a hand to her heart as she took in the image of Addie's mother lying in a pool of blood. "I've never seen this before."

"Neither had I."

Helen glanced over her shoulder. "Oh, Addie, she was so young and so beautiful even in death. How it must hurt you to see her like this."

"It does hurt, but I can't dwell on that now. It's not safe for you to be in this house. The man who lives here could be back any minute, and he's obviously unstable. Please, Helen, just go back to the hospital. I don't want to have to worry about you, too."

Helen seemed not to hear her. Her gaze was still on the grisly images. "She was beautiful, Addie, I admit it. But she was also selfish. You can't imagine. She could be cruel, too. I need you to know that."

Addie's heart fluttered in alarm. "Helen? What are you talking about?"

She turned and met Addie's gaze. Something in her eyes...in her voice...

"She didn't deserve you."

Addie took a step back, her blood icy with shock. "No. Helen, not you..."

"David was wrong earlier. She didn't love you. Not really. She only cared about herself. The last thing she needed was another baby."

"You knew she was pregnant?"

Helen nodded. "I guessed. She didn't deny it."

Addie's hands trembled as she lifted the

weapon. "So you killed her? That doesn't even make sense, Helen." Her gaze went to the photographs. "None of this makes any sense."

"It does if you look at it from my point of view." Helen's voice was soft and smooth and deceptively persuasive. "I loved you like my very own daughter. Cared for you when she didn't have the time or the inclination. She wanted to take you away from me. She wanted you and David all to herself. She was going to give him the family that I never could."

Addie's hand tightened on the weapon. "How could you do such a thing? If you loved me, how could you take my mother away from me?"

"I never wanted to hurt you, sweet girl."

"Don't call me that."

"I don't want to hurt you now. I just want you to understand. I want you to hear my story."

"I'll listen to whatever you have to say, but I'll never understand how you could kill my mother in cold blood. How you could pretend to love me after what you did. You're sick, Helen. You must know that."

Helen's gaze hardened. "A mother does what she has to in order to protect her family."

"You're not my mother."

"I was in all the ways that mattered. You were the child I always wanted and could never have again."

"Again?"

"I had a baby once. I was young and just out of high school. The father left town when he found about the pregnancy. I made the decision to give my son up for adoption. It was the hardest thing I've ever had to do, and I never got over the loss. They say you still feel pain in a severed limb. It's the same with a missing child. Your arms never stop aching. Until you have a baby of your own, you'll never be able to fathom my torment."

"I'm sure it must have been difficult for you," Addie said, willing to placate Helen while she waited for backup.

"Difficult? You've no idea. I told myself I'd done the right thing. He was better off in a good home with two loving parents who could give him everything he needed. But I never forgot him. I never stopped looking for him. And then I met David. He became my whole world, and I thought when we had a child together that I would finally be able to put the past behind me. But years went by, and it never happened for us.

"Then one day I saw you, Addie. I used to walk past your little house on my way to work. Sometimes you would be in the yard playing by yourself or looking out the window at passersby. You were always alone. You seemed so forlorn to me. So starved for a mother's love, and I had so much love to give."

"I had a mother," Addie said. "And she did love me."

"But she loved herself more. She wasn't fit to call herself a mother. I saw how much needed me, so I started stopping by just to say hi. Sandra would sometimes invite me in for a chat. We became friends. She loved that I was so willing to look after you whenever she wanted to go out. She thought I was doing her a favor, but it was the other way around." Helen smiled dreamily. "Our arrangement worked out well for a time. We were all happy. I enjoyed her company, and I came to love you as if you were my own. I couldn't bear the thought of anyone taking you away from me."

"What happened that night?" Addie asked.

"She came to get you at ten, just as she said she would. She was acting very strange that night. Mysterious. She said the two of you might be moving away soon. She was sorry because she knew that I would miss you. The last thing she ever wanted to do was hurt me, but sometimes life happened. That's how she put it. *Life happened.* So cavalier and self-centered. After everything I'd done for her."

"So you lost your temper," Addie said. "It was a crime of passion. I'm just trying to understand how someone I've looked up to and admired, someone I've thought of as family all these years, could do something so unspeakable. You must have been out of your mind with rage."

"Actually, I was calm and resolved," Helen said. "I knew what I had to do. I'd been thinking about it for a while, longer even than I wanted to admit. As it happened, James Merrick was a patient of mine. He'd been coming to see me ever since he arrived in Charleston. I knew about his blackouts, the memory loss, the disorientation. Do you know why memory-regression hypnosis is so unreliable? The subject is completely malleable. Completely susceptible to false memory implantation."

Addie stared at her in horror. "You made him think he killed my mother? You did that to a man who already thought he was losing his mind? You deliberately pushed him over the edge. And then you planted his DNA at the crime scene."

"I did what I had to do," Helen said simply.

"But you overlooked one thing, didn't you? You left your own DNA. What happened? Did you cut yourself in the attack?"

"It wasn't very deep. I never gave it a second thought. The data banks were never going to find a match, because I'd never committed any crimes."

"And then Naomi Quinlan submitted that sample to a public database. And she got a hit." Addie glanced around. "Who lives here, Helen? Who is Daniel Roby?"

"He's my son."

Addie shuddered as she lifted her gaze to the crime-scene photos. "Where is he now?"

Helen's expression turned dreamy again. "I located him some time ago. I didn't know if he'd want to see me, but it turned out that he'd been looking for me, too."

"He sent a sample of his DNA to one of the databases," Addie said.

"Yes. We became close very quickly. It was as if we'd never been apart. He needed me, you see. And I needed him."

Addie lifted her gaze to the photographs. "You told him about my mother?"

"I told him everything. He needed to know that there were people who would try to keep us apart. He came to me as soon as Naomi made contact. We knew she would discover the truth sooner or later, and we'd already lost so much time together. We didn't want to lose each other again."

"So you manipulated him into running her over with his car. Your own son."

Helen's eyes glittered. "My son would do anything for me as I would for him. I won't let anyone take him from me again. Not Naomi Quinlan. Not Ethan Barrow. Not even you, Addie." She turned her head toward the hall but kept her gaze on Addie. "Where are you, Danny?"

A disembodied voice said softly, "I'm here, Mother."

THE GUN IN his back prodded Ethan forward. Hands clasped behind his head, he moved down the hallway and into the front room. Addie's eyes widened at the blood on the side of his face, but the raised weapon in her hand never wavered.

"Drop your gun," Ethan's captor told her. "Do it now or your boyfriend gets a bullet in the brain."

"Don't do it, Addie," Ethan warned. "He'll kill us, anyway."

The man clipped him in the back of his head with the gun so hard Ethan stumbled forward. His captor pushed him to his knees and aimed the barrel at his skull.

"Okay, okay." Addie's gaze was still on Ethan as she bent and placed the gun on the floor.

"Slide it away," the man ordered.

Addie did as she was told. When she straightened, her gaze flicked to Helen. "Does David know you're here? Is he in on this?"

"I don't want to talk about David," she said. "I didn't want any of this to happen. You have to know that. But you left me no choice. You couldn't leave well enough alone."

"So he doesn't know," Addie said. "But he must suspect. That's why he sealed the case files. That's why he questioned Naomi's neighbor about the comings and goings from her house. The weight of those suspicions is what put him in the hospital."

"David is going to be fine," Helen insisted. "I'll find a way to make it up to him."

"Just as you plan to make up all those missing years with your son?" Ethan said as his gaze met

Addie's. "You want to know why he's been following you? All those years of love and attention that Helen lavished on you should have been his. That's why he follows you. That's why he torments you. He's just a jealous little boy."

Roby pressed the gun into Ethan's nape. "Stop talking."

"You're too jealous to realize that your own mother is manipulating you," Ethan taunted. "You think she cares about you? She doesn't. She'll throw you away as soon as you've done her dirty work."

Helen stepped forward, eyes blazing. "That's not true, Danny. Don't listen to him. This is all for you. Everything we're doing is so we can finally be together. Please, son. Stick to the plan. It'll all be over soon."

"Who came up with this plan?" Addie asked as her gaze shifted to Daniel Roby. "Make no mistake, she's already thought this through. She'll put all the blame on you, Danny. Getting rid of Naomi, getting rid of us...it's all part of *her* plan. She'll convince people you're crazy. She'll have you put away just like she did James Merrick."

Helen must have sensed a weakening in her son, because she said quickly, "Just do it. Don't think about it, sweet boy. Just do what has to be done and then set this place on fire. Burn it to the ground so that nothing can be traced back to us. Afterward, go to the cabin and wait for me just as we planned. Do it, Danny. Do it for your mother—"

Her plea was cut off by a loud crash. The front door flew open and Matt Lepear, flanked by two officers, stood with his weapon at the ready as he quickly sized up the situation. Ethan used the diversion to grab Daniel's arm and bring him to the floor. Seizing the gun, he put a foot against Daniel's throat as he took aim.

Meanwhile, Addie lunged for her weapon and then for Helen. The woman collapsed to the floor and buried her face in her hands. "What have I done? Oh, Addie, what have I done?"

"It's a little late to worry about that now." Addie was numb to Helen's remorse. The pain would come later when the dust had settled and yet another loss set in. She turned to Matt. "I see you got my text."

"Yeah, you okay?"

"I'm fine, but Ethan needs the EMTs."

"No, I'm good." He jerked Daniel Roby to his feet and turned him over to one of the officers. Then he crossed the room to Addie. His eyes were dark and deep as he gazed down at her. "Thanks for coming to my rescue."

"Always." For a moment she was mesmerized by that stare. "But we should both thank Matt."

"Damn right," Matt agreed. His gaze went back to the images on the wall. Then he took in Helen's huddled form on the floor. "Is that—"

"Yes."

He shook his head. "What have you gotten yourself into this time?"

"It's a long story," Addie said. "Twenty-five years in the making."

Matt's gaze shifted to Ethan and then back to Addie. "How about you give me the short version."

"In a minute," she murmured as Ethan pulled her into his arms and kissed her.

Chapter Sixteen

The next day, Addie stood on the Battery watching the waves roll in. Behind her, the sun was just setting over the Ashley River, casting a gilded glow over the cityscape. A breeze blew gently across the water, stirring the scent of jasmine from the walled gardens along East Bay. It was the perfect time of day, when shadows lengthened and anticipation settled like a velvety whisper.

She felt his presence before she heard her name. She turned to search the walkway, her gaze moving quickly through the tourists until she found him. He was dressed in his usual dark suit, but he'd taken off his jacket and tie, loosened his collar and rolled up his sleeves. Addie's heart quickened at the sight of him. Like her, he still wore the cuts and bruises that punctuated the end of their investigation. Addie wanted to go to him, to wrap her arms around his waist and lay her head against his shoulder, but she held back. If he was coming to tell her goodbye, she needed to be stoic.

"Thanks for meeting me," he said.

"Of course. I've plenty of time on my hands. You heard Gwen canceled the training session?" When he nodded, Addie said, "I guess she needs time to process everything that's happened."

"I'm sure she's concerned how all this will affect her bottom line, which is probably why she worked so hard to get us to back off the investigation in the first place."

"Do you think she knew your dad was innocent?"

He shrugged. "I don't know. Her ego may not have let her entertain doubts about her profile. In any case, it's over now."

Addie paused. "Did you see your father today?"

"Yes."

"How did it go?"

Ethan stared out over the water for the longest moment. "I knew what to expect. I knew nothing had changed for *him*, and yet a part of me—the kid who watched his hero disintegrate twenty-five years ago—hoped that the truth would somehow set him free."

"You're free," Addie said. "You always believed in his innocence. You never gave up. All those years I thought your father killed my mother. And then to find out that the woman I trusted more than anyone in this world did what she did to your father. Helen and David Cutler were everything to me after my mother died. They helped raised me. It's because of David that I became a cop.

And now I know that he helped cover up Helen's crimes. Out of loyalty and guilt and maybe love, but…" She broke off. "His reasons don't matter. I'm sorry, Ethan. I'm so sorry."

He took her face in his hands. "You've nothing to be sorry about. None of this is on you or me. We were both collateral damage."

"It's a lot to process. I feel like I've lost my family all over again."

He gazed down into her eyes. "You're not alone, Addie."

Her heart started to pound. "I don't want you to worry about me, okay? I'll be fine."

"What if I want to worry about you? What if I don't want to be alone?" He dropped his hands to his sides and turned back to the water as if were suddenly unsure of himself. "There's an opening in the field office here in Charleston. I'm considering putting in for a transfer."

Addie laid her hand on his arm. "Don't do that. Not for me. You'd kill your career with that transfer."

"Someone wise once told me that a career is not the worst thing a person can lose." He turned back to her, his gaze earnest. "I'm not asking for a commitment. I'm just asking for another chance."

She closed her eyes and let the breeze and his voice wash over her. "Welcome home, Ethan."

* * * * *